THE HAWK AND THE DOVE

THE HAWK AND THE DOVE

Penelope Wilcock

CROSSWAY BOOKS • WHEATON, ILLINOIS
A DIVISION OF GOOD NEWS PUBLISHERS

*For David Bowes
with deep gratitude*

The Hawk and the Dove.

Copyright © 1990 by Penelope Wilcock.

U.S. edition published by Crossway Books, a division of
Good News Publishers, Wheaton, Illinois 60187.

First British edition 1990 (Minstrel, a division of Monarch Publications Ltd.);
first U.S. edition 1991 (Crossway Books).

Cover illustration: Chuck Gillies

First printing, 1991

Printed in the United States of America

Library of Congress Cataloging-in-Publication Data
Wilcock, Penelope.
    The Hawk and the Dove / Penelope Wilcock. — 1st U.S. ed.
      p.   cm.
    "First British edition 1990 (Minstrel, a division of Monarch
Publications Ltd.)"—T.p. verso.
    I. Title
PR6073.I394H39   823'.914—dc20   90-19779
ISBN 0-89107-602-6

99		98		97		96		95		94		93		92		91
15	14	13	12	11	10	9	8	7	6	5	4	3	2

CONTENTS

I
MOTHER

I wish you had known my mother. I remember, as clearly as if it were yesterday, toiling up the hill at the end of the school day, towards the group of mothers who stood at the crest of the rise, waiting to collect their children from the county primary school where my little sisters went.

The mothers chatted together, plump and comfortable, wearing modest, flowery dresses, pretty low-heeled sandals, their hair curled and tinted, and just that little bit of make-up to face the world in. Some had pushchairs with wriggling toddlers. Together, they smiled and nodded and gossipped and giggled, young and friendly and kind .... But there at the top of the hill, at a little distance from all the rest, stood my mother, as tall and straight and composed as a prophet, her great blue skirt flapping in the breeze, her thick brown hair tumbling down her back. By her side stood my littlest sister, her hand nestling confidingly in my mother's hand, her world still sheltered in the folds of that blue skirt from the raw and bewildering society of the playground.

My mother. She was not a pretty woman, and never thought to try and make herself so. She had an uncompromising chin, firm lips, a nose like a hawk's beak and unnerving grey eyes. Eyes that went straight past the outside of you and into the middle, which meant that you could relax about the torn jersey, the undone shoe

7

laces, the tangled hair and the unwashed hands at the dinner table, but you had to feel very uncomfortable indeed about the stolen sweets, the broken promise, and the unkind way you ran away from a little sister striving to follow you on her short legs. My mother. Often, after tea, she would stand, having cleared away the tea things, at the sink, just looking out of the windows at the seagulls riding the air-currents on the evening sky; her hands still, her work forgotten, a faraway expression in her eyes.

Therese and I would do our homework after tea, sitting at the tea-table in the kitchen. The three little ones would play out of doors until the light was failing, and then Mother would call them in, littlest first, and bath them in the lean-to bathroom at the back of the kitchen, brush their hair and clean their teeth, help them on with their nightgowns, and tuck them in to bed.

This was the moment of decision for Therese and me. Ours was a little house in a terrace of shabby houses that clung to a hillside by the sea, and we had only two bedrooms, so all five of us sisters slept in the same room on mattresses side by side on the floor. Mother hated electric light—she said it assaulted the sleepy soul and drove the sandman away, and when the little ones were ready for bed, she would tuck in Mary and Beth, and light the candle and sit down with Cecily, the littlest one, in the low comfortable chair in the corner of the room. If she put them to bed and left them, there would be pandemonium. Cecily would not stay in bed at all and romped gaily about the room, and Beth and Mary would begin to argue, starting with a simple remark like 'Beth, I can't get to sleep with you sniffing,' and finishing with a general commotion of crying and quarrelling.

So Mother resigned herself to stay with them as they fell asleep, and she sat, with the littlest one snuggled on her lap, in the room dimly glowing with candle-light, softly astir with the breathing and sighing and turning over of children settling for the night.

Therese and I, at sixteen and fourteen years old, had to choose between staying alone downstairs to read a book, or paint or gaze into the fire; and creeping upstairs with the little ones, to sit with Mother in the candle-light, and listen to her lullabies.

Most often, Therese stayed down, but I crept upstairs to Mother and lay on my bed, gazing at the candle as the flame dipped and rose with the draught, watching the shadows as they trembled and moved about the ceiling. After a while, as we kept our quiet, shadowy vigil, I would whisper, 'Mother, tell me a story.'

So I wish you had known my mother. I wish you could hear the stories she told in her quiet, thoughtful voice. I wish I could take you into the magic of that breathing, candle-lit room, which she filled with people and strange ways from long ago. I wish I could remember all of them to tell you, but years have gone by now, and I am not sure of everything she said. But for the times you, too, have a quiet moment, and need to unhook your mind from the burden of the day, here are some of the stories my mother told me. They are the stories she told me the year I turned fifteen.

I was just beginning to ask questions, to search for a way of looking at things that would make sense. The easy gaiety and simple sorrows of childhood had been swallowed up and lost in a hungry emptiness, a search for meaning that nothing seemed to satisfy. At school, I was only a number, a non-person. They could answer my questions about the theory of relativity and whether it was permissible in modern English to split an infinitive: but when it came to the great, lonely yearning that was opening up inside me, they didn't seem even to want to hear the question, let alone try to answer it. I went to church every Sunday, and I listened to what they said about Jesus, and I believed it all, I really did; but was there anyone anywhere who cared about it enough to behave as if it were true? I felt disenchanted.

I began to wonder, as spring wore on to summer in

that, my fifteenth year, if I would ever meet anyone who could look me in the eye, who could say sorry without making a joke of it, who could cry without embarrassment, have a row and still stay friends. As for mentioning the word 'love', well ... it provoked sniggers, not much else. The hunger of it all ached inside me. Maybe Mother knew. Maybe she could guess what I never told her, could not even tell myself; that I was desperate for something more than smiles and jokes and surfaces; that I was beginning to wonder if it was possible to stretch out your hand in the darkness and find it grasped by another hand, not evaded, rejected, or ignored.

Mother said these stories were true, and I never knew her tell a lie ... but then you could never be quite sure what she meant by 'truth'; fact didn't always come into it.

II
FATHER COLUMBA

When I was a girl, a bit younger than you (my mother began) I had someone to tell me stories, too. It wasn't my mother who told me stories though, it was my great-grandmother, and her name was Melissa, like yours. Great-grandmother Melissa told me all sorts of stories, stories about my uncles and cousins, about my great-aunt Alice who was a painter and lived in a little stone cottage at Bell Busk in Yorkshire. Old Aunt Alice's cottage was one of a row of terraced cottages, all the same except that Aunt Alice's was painted in psychedelic colours.

Great-grandmother Melissa told me about my auntie's duck that had four legs – and she took me to see it too. She told me about one of my far-off ancestors, who was found on the doorstep as a tiny baby, in a shopping bag. She told me about my cousin's dog Russ, who bit off a carol-singer's finger, and about my grandfather's dog that had to be put down because it loved him so much it went out one night and killed twenty hens and piled them all up on his doorstep. She told me about how she and her sisters took it in turns to pierce each others' ears with a needle and a cork, and socks stuffed in their mouths to stop them screaming, so that their mother wouldn't find out what they'd done. All kinds of tales she told me, and all about our family. But the ones I liked best were about a monastery long ago. These

11

stories had been handed down, grandmother to grand-daughter, for seven hundred years. They came from a long ago Great-uncle Edward, who lived to be nearly a hundred, and was a very wise old man.

At the end of his life, when his blue eyes were faded and his skin was wrinkled, and his hair reduced to white wisps about his bald head (although he had the bushiest of eyebrows and whiskers that grew down his nose), Uncle Edward would while away his days telling stories to his visitors. The one who had the stories from him was his great-niece—*she* was a Melissa too. This Melissa began handing down the stories, and they came down through the generations until my great-grandmother, in the evening of her life, as she came into the twilight, would sit with me and tell me that long ago Uncle Edward's stories. And now I will tell them to you, Melissa.

Great-uncle Edward was a monk, at the Benedictine abbey of St Alcuin, on the edge of the Yorkshire moors. He had been a wandering friar in the order of the blessed Francis of Assisi, and had spent his life roaming the countryside, preaching the gospel. But as time went by, and his sixtieth birthday came and went, he felt a need for a more settled life. So after forty years of preaching throughout the English shires, he entered the community of Benedictines at St Alcuin's Abbey in Yorkshire, far away from his family home near Ely, but just as cold and windy. Great-uncle Edward (now Brother Edward) was made the infirmarian of the abbey—that is to say, he took care of the monks when they were ill—for in his wandering days with the Franciscan friars, he had picked up a wealth of healing lore. He was skilled in the use of tisanes and poultices, herbal salves and spiced wines and aromatic oils, and he could set a bone or repair a wound as well as any man. So he settled down at St Alcuin's, and gave himself to the work of nursing the sick and caring for the old under the Rule of Life of St Benedict.

In the year 1303—Brother Edward's sixty-sixth —when he had been four years at the abbey, the good old man who was the abbot of the monastery died peacefully in his sleep with a smile on his face, over-burdened with years and glad to enter into the peace of the blessed. The brothers were sorry to lose him, for he had ruled them gently, with kindness and authority, knowing how to mingle mercy with justice so as to get the best out of his flock and lead them in their life of work and prayer. The sorriest of all was Father Chad, the prior of the monastery, second-in-command under the abbot, upon whose shoulders now fell the burden of responsibility for the community until they had a new abbot. Father Chad was a shy, quiet man, a man of prayer, a man of few words—a gentle, retiring man. He was not a leader of men. He had no idea why he had been chosen to be prior and was horrified to find the greatness of the abbacy thrust upon him. With a small sigh of regret he left the snug prior's cell, which was built against the warm chimney of the brothers' community room, the warming room, and installed himself in the large, draughty apartment which was the abbot's lodging. Day and night he prayed that God would send a new abbot soon, and day and night he prayed that they wouldn't choose him.

It was the usual thing, when the abbot of the monastery died, for the brothers to elect from among their number the new lord abbot. The brothers of St Alcuin's prayed hard, and the more senior of the brethren spent long hours in council; but though they prayed long and considered earnestly, they came reluctantly to the con-clusion that there was no brother among them with the necessary qualities of leadership to follow in the old abbot's footsteps. So they appealed to the bishop to choose them a new superior from among the brothers of another monastery, and said they would abide by his choice and accept whomever he sent to rule over them.

Before too long, word came from the bishop that he

would himself be presenting their new superior to them. Since he had to travel through their part of the world on his return home to Northumbria from a conference with the king in London, he would visit them on his way, bringing their new abbot with him. The abbey reverberated with excitement, all except for Father Chad, who dreaded playing host to both a bishop and an abbot.

Great-uncle Edward did his best to encourage him; 'Put a brave face on it, Father Prior! Chin up, never say die. 'Tis only one night when all's said and done, then you'll be back to your cosy nook by the warming-room flues and leave this windy barn to the new man, God help him. The bishop gives you his name in that letter, does he?'

Father Chad looked at the letter from the bishop, not that he needed to. He had read and re-read it a dozen times this morning, and knew the contents of it near enough by heart now; but he ran his finger down the script to make sure.

'Here. Father Columba, the sub-prior from St Peter's near Ely. He says very little about him. We shall have to wait and see.'

'Ely? I was born and bred on the fens near Ely. My nephew took the cowl at St Peter's. I wonder ... Columba, you say? Columba the dove. No. No, wouldn't be him. No sane man would have named that lad after a dove!'

'You'll eat with us, Edward, when they come tonight?' Father Chad tried to sound casually friendly, but Edward knew panic when he saw it.

'I shall count myself honoured. I'll go now and get my chores done early. There's old Father Lucanus suffering with the pain in his shoulder and neck again. I must spend some time with him, give him a rub with aromatics. It eases the ache wonderfully.' Brother Edward stood up slowly and strolled across the bare, comfortless room to the great oak door. He paused in the doorway and looked back. Father Chad still sat in the imposing carved chair, staring gloomily at the letter on the huge, heavy table before him.

'Time and the hour outrun the longest day, Father Chad,' said Brother Edward consolingly. 'It'll be over before you know it.'

He set off to the infirmary, well content with the prospect of being among the first to have a good look at the new abbot.

'Columba.' He tried out the sound of the name, thoughtfully. 'Columba. Irishman, maybe? We shall see.'

When a man entered as a brother in the monastic life (my mother explained) he had done with the world and its ways and set out as though on a brand new life to try and live in every way, with a single heart, for God. He took three vows; one of poverty, that he would never have anything to call his own again; one of chastity, that he would never have a wife or a girlfriend, but all women would be like sisters to him, just as all men would be like brothers; and one of obedience, that he would submit to the authority of the abbot of the community, and obey his word in everything. When he made his first vows after six months as a novice, the monk would be clothed in the habit of the order, which was a long robe—black for the Benedictines—with a separate hood called a cowl, and wide sleeves and a leather belt.

To show that he really had finished with all the trappings of his old life, the monk was given a new name by his abbot, as if he were a brand new person. The abbot usually tried to pick something appropriate to the man's character or background. Great-uncle Edward had been christened Edward as a baby, after King Edward the Confessor, who was a good and holy king. When he entered the religious life, his abbot said he should keep the same name, since no one could hope to be more devoted to the Lord Jesus than King Edward had been. And now the man the bishop was bringing was Columba, named after the Irish Saint. Columba, the dove, the bird that represents gentleness and kindness and simplicity, as well as being a symbol of the Holy Spirit of God.

After Vespers Brother Edward hurried with anticipation to the abbot's lodging to meet their distinguished supper-guests, who had ridden in an hour ago and been welcomed to the guest house.

'Well, well!' murmured Brother Edward, as his new abbot entered the room: for it was indeed the son of his sister Melissa, whom he had not seen for years.

'Columba!' Edward chuckled to himself. 'Meek and gentle dove, eh? Well, I shall be very surprised ...'

The new abbot, whom Edward had known since babyhood, was certainly no dove. His mother, dead now, had been a proud, noble lady, and his father was a rich and powerful Norman aristocrat with a face as proud as an eagle and a grip on all that was his as fierce as the grip of an eagle's talons. When their child was born, he had a little beaky nose like a bird of prey, and a flashing dark eye quite startling in a pink baby face. His mother, laughing, called him Peregrine, and well named he was, for like a hawk he grew: fierce, proud and arrogant, with a piercing look and a hawk's beaky nose. Great-grandmother Melissa said I favoured him in my looks, even all these years later.

This Peregrine had two older brothers. The elder of the two, Geoffroi, took charge of the farming side of his father's estate. Emmanuel, the second brother, went for a soldier. Peregrine, youngest, stubbornest, fiercest of the three, surprised them all by losing his proud, stubborn heart to the Lord our Saviour, turning his back on the world and entering as a novice at St Peter's Abbey near Ely, to try the monastic life as a Benedictine brother.

Of course, it's one thing to love Jesus and quite another to follow him; and poverty, chastity and obedience sat about as comfortably on Peregrine as his hair shirt. Still, the brothers saw promise in him, and as much from stubbornness as anything else he grimly struggled through his novitiate year, finally making his vows and being professed as Brother Columba—a name which showed either that his abbot had a wry sense of humour or else that he had greater faith than most men and no sense of humour at all.

Peregrine was a good scholar and a devout monk, and he was ordained a priest, too. He was also a brilliant philosopher, and had inherited from his father a shrewd business mind and unmistakable qualities of leadership. He was not a popular man, because although he was just and upright and true, there was precious little compassion or gentleness about him. The fight to discipline himself, to attain all the spiritual and intellectual targets he set himself, occupied all his energies, leaving nothing to help him learn the gentler art of loving, much less of allowing himself to be loved. Still, he was valued for his abilities, even if he inspired little affection, and he was given several positions of responsibility.

When the bishop consulted the abbot of St Peter's, to see if their community had anyone who could be sent to St Alcuin's to serve as abbot, Father Columba had only recently been made sub-prior. The abbot of St Peter's suggested him at once, and so Peregrine was sent, at the beginning of his forty-fifth year, as Lord Abbot to the monastery of St Alcuin in the north of Yorkshire. The bishop was satisfied that Peregrine would serve them well. He had listened to the advice of the abbot of St Peter's, who knew the monks in his care better than they knew themselves:

'He's ruthless with himself, always has been. Drives the men under him hard too; but he's fair-minded, unfailingly courteous and astute, nobody's fool. He's a solitary man. I've wondered, sometimes, if he's lonely, but it's hard to say. Just your stiff, formal, courtly French nobleman, I think. We'll not break our hearts to see him go, and yet I shall be sorry in a way to lose him. There's a shining, honourable love of God about him that's a rare thing to see. Abbot Columba. Yes, he'll wear it well.'

So the bishop brought him to St Alcuin's, and Brother
Edward watched with amused sympathy as the prior
greeted them. The nails of Chad's fingers were bitten to
the quick, and his left eye was twitching as he welcomed
them with the kiss of peace and played host to them at
the abbot's table. The senior brethren of the abbey
dined with them, as did the bishop's chaplain.

Mingled in the company, Brother Edward was able to
study his nephew well. Father Columba had seemed
pleased to see his uncle again, embracing him with a
smile of pleasure and surprise, the sudden, vivid smile
that Edward remembered in him as a boy irradiating his
features with unexpected warmth.

Now, as Father Columba ate and talked, unmoved by
the eyes of the brethren upon him, Brother Edward
observed him thoughtfully. He looked at the piercing
intelligence of the dark eyes, the controlled intensity of
his manner, the impatient movements of his hands. 'Like
his father, Frenchman to the core,' thought Edward.
'Henri always talked more with his hands than with
words. He's grown as imperious and autocratic as his
father too. Columba, my eye! They should have stuck
with Peregrine. Dear me, yes. Poor old Chad. This man
is going to come as a shock after our last abbot.'

Brother Edward thought it was a huge joke that his
nephew Peregrine had been renamed Columba, and he
was still chuckling at the thought of it the next day as
he made the beds and washed and shaved the aged
brothers in his care in the infirmary. Brother John, who
was his assistant, asked him what he was laughing at,
and Edward told him how their new abbot had been
Peregrine, the bird of prey, before he became Columba,
the dove. Brother John grinned hugely. Word got
round, and it was not long before it was the joke of the
whole community, and the new abbot was called 'Father
Peregrine' behind his back, and 'Father Columba' to his
face and to visitors.

The brothers of St Alcuin's found their new superior

rather unapproachable, his remote and reserved courtesy contrasting unfavourably with the old abbot's kindness. They found Father Peregrine's imperious face and noble carriage intimidating, though they were cautiously proud of him, too. He proved to be a good and competent abbot, and ruled over his monastery with justice and integrity, commanding the respect and loyalty of the brothers, who would not, in any case, have dared to question his aristocratic authority.

A year went by, and the brothers began to grow accustomed to their new superior. Another year and they had almost forgotten what it was like before he came. It was Easter, two years after Father Peregrine had come to be their abbot. Easter, the greatest feast of the Christian year, and all the local people had come up to the abbey, and the guest house was full of pilgrims come to celebrate the feast of the Resurrection. So many people, so many processions, so much music! So many preparations to be made by the singers, the readers, those who served at the altar and those who served in the guest house, not to mention those who worked in the kitchens and the stables. The abbey was bursting with guests, neighbours, relatives and strangers.

The Easter Vigil was mysterious and beautiful, with the imagery of fire and water and the Paschal candle lit in the great, vaulted dimness of the abbey church. Brother Gilbert the precentor's voice mounted joyfully in the triumphant beauty of the *Exultet*; all the bells rang out for the risen Lord, and the voices of the choirboys from the abbey school soared with heart-breaking loveliness in the music declaring the risen life of Jesus. Easter Day itself was radiant with sunshine for once, as well as celebration. Oh, the joyful splendour of a church crammed full of people, a thundering of voices singing 'Credo—I believe.'

The newest of the novices, Brother Thomas, known to the other novices as Brother Tom, who had just two weeks ago taken his first vows, stood almost dazed, transported by the beauty of the celebration. He had been in the community only six months, having entered once his father's harvest was safely gathered in, in the autumn of 1305. His father, a big, strapping, red-faced man, a Yorkshire farmer born and bred, had accompanied him to the abbey. His mother they had left in tears at home. She had only two children, both sons, and they were her whole life. In addition to this, the farm could ill do without the sons' labour and management. But God calls whom he will, and devout Christians both, the lad's parents respected and supported his wish to try the religious life.

With an almost oppressive sense of awe, the two men had entered through the little portal set in the massive gates of the abbey enclosure. They were put at their ease again by the kindly welcome of Brother Cyprian, the old porter, who had chatted comfortably to them as he escorted them to the abbot's lodging. His broad Yorkshire accent was something of home in this imposing place. 'Tha munnot fear Father Abbot, lad. He's not an easy man, but he's a good man for all that. Tha mun speak up for thyself, for he'll not bite thee. Through here, this is our refectory. Through yon door into t' cloister, aye, that's it. ... Now then, here we are, this is Father's house.'

What Brother Thomas remembered most of his first meeting with Abbot Peregrine (apart from the dark grey eyes that looked as if they could read his mind) was the quick, eloquent gesturing of his hands, the way he drummed his fingers thoughtfully on the table as he looked at him and weighed him up. In the abbot's hands all his vitality, his restless energy seemed concentrated, and the lad was fascinated by the long, fine, strong, restless fingers, so different from his own. He looked down at his hands, broad and work-hard, rough and weathered already at nineteen years old, and reposeful with the peace you so often see in a farmer's hands. They rested on his thighs as he listened in tranquillity to his father discussing him with the abbot.

'... and you can spare him, from the farm?' the abbot was asking his father, probing. 'Only two sons, you say? You can afford to let one of them go?'

The farmer met the abbot's questioning gaze. 'He's not cut out for the land, not this one, Father. Neither use nor ornament to me is this lad, when his heart's elsewhere. Any road, we shall see. I'd not wonder if the fire dies down before long. He's a mighty trencherman— well, look at him, he's built like an ox, both of my lads are—and he'll leave a few broken hearts behind him among the lasses when he's gone. To be honest with you, I cannot see him creeping about in silence or telling beads on his knees. As demure and quiet as young ladies are some of your brothers here, and that my lad will never be. But let him try it if he will. There's always a welcome for him with his mother and me should it all come to nothing.'

This was the longest, most personal speech the farmer had ever made, and he took out his linen handkerchief and wiped the beads of sweat from his forehead as he finished. A smile twitched the corners of the abbot's mouth. He was amused by the description of his monks. He was himself inclined to be irritable with the more timid and submissive men. The abbot turned his gaze on the farmer's son, who returned it calmly, but felt somehow belittled and exposed by the aristocratic amusement with which he was regarded.

'He thinks I am a peasant, and beneath him,' he thought, somewhat resentfully, and stoutly endured the abbot's scrutiny.

'What say you then, my son?' asked Father Peregrine. 'Your father has little hope of your staying the course, it seems. It is a hard life. I shall think no less of you if you wish to change your mind.'

The abbot's aloof, ironic manner nettled the lad; the educated voice with its slight French inflection grated on him. He spoke up impulsively, with some heat. 'I doubt you could think much less of me than you do now, my lord, anyway. I am a common working man, not of your kind.'

'Eh, then. Now, now!' expostulated his father. 'That's uncivil, lad! Mind who you're talking to!' But the abbot ignored him and looked steadily at the young man, serious now.

'Well, then? You are minded to enter with us?'

'I am, my lord.'

And standing here in the sunshine and soaring music of Easter Day, Brother Thomas was glad and sure, at peace to his very soul. This was where he belonged.

'*Credo in unum Deum*—I believe in one God—oh, yes!'

The next day, Easter Monday, most of the guests were leaving, and there was much coming and going, saddling of horses, saying of goodbyes. It was next to impossible to find anyone or get anything done. The place was in turmoil. After Vespers, as the sun was sinking, Brother Edward was sent with a message in search of Father Matthew, the novice master.

Edward went into the great abbey church, determined that this would be his last task before he sat down wearily for a bite to eat with the other brothers—and then Compline and bed. He was fairly confident he would find Father Matthew in the sacristy adjoining the choir, making sure Brother Thomas knew how to set out vessels and vestments for the Mass in the morning, putting ready the Communion bread, and marking the places in the holy books for the celebrant.

Brother Edward cut through the Lady chapel—the quickest way—and although by this hour it was all but dark in the church, he walked swiftly: partly because he was in a hurry, and partly because this was his home and he knew his way about as well in dusk as in daylight.

He was striding purposefully up the little aisle, peering ahead to see if he could make out a glimmer of light from the sacristy that would indicate Father Matthew's presence within, when unexpectedly he drove his foot into a bulky obstacle across his path, and all but lost his balance. From the floor came a deep, inhuman groan of agony, like an animal, like something in the torment of hell.

Brother Edward's scalp crawled, and gooseflesh stood out all over his body at the sound. His mouth went dry, and his hands trembled as he bent in the gloom to peer at and feel the bundle at his feet. As his hand moved over it, again came that groan: hideous, wordless in anguish. Brother Edward, thoroughly shaken, hesitated a moment and then decided to go for help, and a light.

Edging his way round whoever or whatever it was, he ran to the sacristy, where he found Father Matthew, as he had expected, laying out vestments with Brother Thomas. They looked up, startled, at Edward's white, agitated face.

'Brother, for God's sake, come,' he gasped. 'Bring a light, make haste.'

Father Matthew asked no questions, but snatched up a candle and followed him, and together they hurried back into the Lady chapel, while Brother Thomas followed a little uncertainly, sensing trouble and not sure if he was expected to help or mind his own business. As he crossed the sacristy, he saw that Brother Edward's sandal had left behind a trail of marks, and the one on the threshold of the room reflected the light a little. Frowning, he bent down and held the light to look closer.

'Mother of God, it's blood!' he murmured, and carrying the light in his hand followed his superiors out into the Lady chapel.

There they found Abbot Peregrine, though his face was bruised and beaten almost beyond recognition. His body was tied and bound with his knees drawn up to his chin and his hands behind his back, the right side of his face laid open in a ragged gash that exposed his cheekbone and extended from his temple nearly to his jaw. Blood had flowed from his nose into his mouth and mingled with blood from a split lip. Two of his teeth were spat out on the floor in a sticky puddle of blood.

Appalled, the brothers looked at each other.

'Who can have done this?' whispered Father Matthew, but Edward shook his head.

'So many strangers, so many guests. Did you not hear anything in the sacristy?'

'Nothing, Brother. We came in through the main body of the church, not through here, just ten minutes before you found us. We saw no one. Whoever it was must have fled, because—'

'All right, all right,' interrupted Brother Edward. 'Brother Thomas, find me something to cut these ropes with, the knife in my belt will be too blunt to do it carefully.'

Thomas ran off without a word, and Brother Edward gently felt Peregrine's back and skull to be sure it was safe to move him. His hair was sticky with blood, and there was a swollen, spongy bruise, but his skull was intact. Thomas returned with a small knife, very sharp, filched from the kitchen, and Brother Edward took it from him and bent to cut the ropes that bound the abbot's arms behind his back.

'Lift the light a little, Matthew. I can't see what I'm doing. Oh, but what's this!?'

Peregrine's hands, tied behind him, were smashed and mangled, grotesquely broken, disfigured and bruised. Gingerly, Edward cut the cords that bound him. They moved the benches aside and carefully laid him straight, and Edward felt all over him for broken bones.

'That's his collar-bone broken. Two ribs here. No, three. Hold the light steady, Matthew, let me look at his leg. No, his left leg, that's it. His shin-bone's smashed, look at this. That'll never set straight. His knee too. Brother, what kind of devilish beast can have done this to him? And why? Dear Lord, what hatred! Nothing else broken, though. Brother Thomas, run to the infirmary and ask Brother John for a stretcher. Quick as you can.'

He sat back on his heels and looked down at the still, battered body.

'Matthew, I kicked him,' he said. 'I came through in a hurry, and I stumbled over him. The moan of pain that came from him, I've never heard anything like it. He was lying here like this, and I kicked him. Still, thank God he's alive, poor soul.'

Brother Thomas came back bringing a stretcher and with him Brother John from the infirmary. As gently as they could, they eased him onto it.

'Brother, have a care for his hands. They may be beyond repairing, but we'll not injure them further. Cross his arms so, that's right. Now then, gently.'

They carried him to the infirmary, and he lay there as still as a corpse, his eyes swollen shut with bruising, his breath snoring in the oozing blood of his nose.

Until dawn, Edward tended to the broken mess of his hands, fine, scholar's hands, shattered now. He made wooden splints, and set the bones and bound them straight, but knew with a heavy heart that those hands would never serve again to do fine lettering. He had set the leg bone as well as he could, but it was smashed, not broken clean, and he doubted if it would ever bear a man's weight again. He set and bandaged the ribs and the collar-bone, too, and then washed and bound the other wounds, salving the bruises with ointments, and laying green poultices on the places where the skin was split. The hideous wound on his face he repaired as best he could. As the sun rose on the following day Edward sank down on his knees and prayed, offering up the work he had done, beseeching the Great Physician to make it good, to bring healing where his own skill fell short.

They thought Peregrine might die. By the mercy of God his skull and his back were not broken, but the men who had beaten him had left him for dead. However, he did not die, though for a long time he lay without motion or speech, unable to open his eyes. Brother Edward and Brother John took turns to watch him night and day, and Father Chad took up the responsibilities of abbot once again.

That first day, they began by dripping water through his lips from a soaked cloth. Then after two days, as the bruises began to subside a little, they were able to feed him broth and honeyed wine; slowly, slowly dribbling it in through the split, swollen mouth. It was impossible to say if he was in his senses or not, for he made no response to them at all. All the same, they talked to him gently and reassuringly, explaining what was happening to him, words of comfort and love. He was able to swallow most of the soup and wine they fed him, which Brother Edward saw as a sign of hope, but he did not speak to them for three days. By this time the swelling had eased, and his face was recognisable as his, in spite of the bruises and the gash down the right side. Brother Edward was fearful he might have suffered some internal injury, for there was bruising on his belly and back, but though he saw some blood in his water the first day or two, he seemed to have sustained remarkably little damage. They did not attempt to lift him to go to the privy, and he had to be cleaned like a baby.

They had just finished washing him on the Thursday morning, the third day they had been nursing him, when he spoke to them for the first time. He said, 'Thank you.'

Like the other brothers, Brother Edward had respected—but had no especial affection for—their austere, uncompromising abbot, despite his blood-relationship. But nursing that battered body and fighting for him in intercession, he had come to care passionately what became of him. Day and night, he and Brother John had taken turns to watch over the suffering man.

A flood of relief and joy and love welled up in Edward as he raised his head and met Peregrine's eyes, which were open at last. He saw the look in those eyes change from a bleak gaze of hopeless pain to wonder at his own face so full of love and relief. Compassion mingled with the relief as Edward saw that the man was astonished to find himself loved. He always remembered the amazement in Peregrine's eyes as the abbot found the love he had never inspired, never won, now given him as a gift in the midst of his helplessness and pain.

In the end, it was that love which pulled him through the horror of what had happened to him, and of his helplessness. His proud, independent soul writhed at the humiliation of being fed and cleaned like a baby and recoiled from the prospect of facing life with maimed hands and a useless leg. He spoke little, and complained not at all. 'Thank you,' were the words most often on his lips.

Though he seemed calm and self-possessed, Edward, knowing him from childhood, guessed at the howling terror inside, and would sit and say the Office with him and talk to him about the comings and goings of the abbey. He sat quietly beside him at night, too, when Peregrine slept restlessly, sometimes starting awake with a sob of fear. Beyond that, Edward felt powerless to help him, did not know how to reach through his abbot's reserve to the terror inside, and comfort him.

As soon as he was able to eat, they propped him up to feed him, but he still couldn't feed himself because his hands were splinted and bound.

Brother Edward asked him if he knew why he had been so savagely attacked, and he said yes, he knew. The words came painfully.

'Many years ago now, there was one Will Godricson, who worked on my father's estate. You probably won't remember him, Edward; you were with the Franciscans by then. He killed a man in a drunken brawl. My father handed him over to justice, and he was hanged. He was a violent man to the point of insanity, and they could scarcely hold him on the day he was taken away. They bound him, in the end, bound him with his hands behind his back, his feet together and his knees drawn up to his chin. His two young sons were standing there watching; poor, scared ragamuffins, exposed to it all. They were brought up in violence, and they pledged themselves to vengeance on my father for their father's life. They never found a way to carry it out on him; you know him, well guarded and well armed, he always carried a dagger and knew how to use it. But it must have come to their ears eventually that a son of that household lived here, accessible to visitors and without defence. I suppose they came with the crowd and waited their moment.

'I had been into the sacristy in search of Father Matthew; but not finding him there, I came out through the Lady chapel, where they were waiting for me. They must have followed me into the church. They approached me, and I greeted them. They seemed vaguely familiar, though it was dusk, and they were but children when I saw them last. They had the look of their father. One of them carried a club, which seemed strange, but then visitors departing on a journey need some defence in the moors and wild places. They ... they said ....' He stopped, his voice unsteady, bit his lip and continued, 'I ... they. ...' But his voice died to a whisper, and he closed his eyes and shook his head.

Edward laid a gentling hand on his arm, 'No, no, lad, no need. Your body tells its own story.' And beyond that, the tale was never told.

The day came when he was mended as well as he ever would be, and ready to take up his responsibilities as abbot of the monastery again. The collar-bone and ribs had knitted nicely, but the leg was stiff and crooked for ever, and as Edward had predicted, the shin-bone was too damaged to take his weight, so that ever afterwards he used a crutch to get about. It had to be a crutch, and not a stick, because in spite of Brother Edward's best efforts, Father Peregrine's hands were misshapen and twisted. He had stretched them out to defend himself against the club, and to save himself as he was knocked to the ground, and in their cruel, insane vengeance, his attackers had stamped on them in their heavy labourers' clogs: not once, but again and again and again.

The brothers were unsure how to behave towards him when first he came among them again. It was as though their abbot had been taken away, and this was a new person. Used to the imperious, aristocratic, decisive figure they had known, with his swift, purposeful stride and his hands gesturing impatience, they were appalled by the look of him. He had grown very thin, his face disfigured by the livid scar, his eyes shadowed with pain. His hands were good for almost nothing now, and although he did not try to conceal them, he no longer moved them as he talked, but kept them still. He went every day to the infirmary, at Brother Edward's insistence, so that Edward might massage the broken hands with his healing aromatic oils, and help him exercise them. Yet though he could feed himself, albeit slowly and with difficulty, and write, though laboriously and untidily, he would never again work on fine manuscript illumination, or sit late at night writing essays, sermons and poems. He could not even cut up his food or fasten his own sandals, and the hands tended to cramp into claws if Brother Edward left off his care of them for any length of time.

Peregrine's progress about the place was slow, lame and awkward, painful to watch. There were those who wondered if a man so broken would be fit to continue as abbot of a monastery, but they bided their time and gave him his chance. They found him changed in other ways, too. The old arrogance and self-assurance had been knocked out of him, and he was humbly grateful for the help his brothers gave him to turn pages and cut food. The constant need for help in everyday things brought him closer to the brothers, and the quietly spoken 'Thank you, brother', with an appreciative smile, were what they had gained in exchange for the imposing figure they had lost. Uncle Edward said that few of the brothers guessed just what it cost Peregrine to come among them again, disfigured and clumsy and slow.

Brother Thomas was one of those few. He had helped to carry Father Peregrine to the infirmary that Easter Monday night, and then wandered away to sit on his own in his cell, no longer needed in the infirmary, but with no stomach for company. Every time he closed his eyes, he saw the limp body, beaten almost senseless, broken and bloodied. Every time he opened his eyes, he saw the tortured man hanging on the crucifix on the wall of his cell. He couldn't decide which was worse. In the end he sat staring at the floor until the bell rang for Compline, when he rose automatically to his feet and went down to the chapel. He sat through the Office in a daze, and was glad of the shelter of the Great Silence as he walked numbly back to his cell afterwards.

Late, late that night as he lay awake on his lumpy bed, unable to sleep, he could not expunge from his mind the sight of those hands: destroyed, hopelessly mangled, swollen, bleeding, lacerated. He felt sick at the memory. He stared into the darkness, thinking of the cool self-possession of the man, the resolute, intelligent face, the eyes with their almost fanatical intensity, the proud bearing of him; but above all he thought of those quick, impatient, clever hands—oh, smashed. The brutality chilled him.

Even that memory failed to prepare Brother Thomas for the change in Father Peregrine when he came back into the community again; the painful toil of his progress about the abbey, the way his ironic superiority had been snuffed out as if it had never been. Most of all Brother Thomas looked in horror and pity at the silenced hands, scarred and twisted, which Father Peregrine did not attempt to hide, but which no longer spoke in gesture and impatience as he talked. They were still now, bearing their own mute testimony to his suffering.

'How can he bear it?' said Brother Thomas to Brother Francis, his friend in the novitiate, as they went in to the chapter house together, on the last day of April, the day Father Peregrine officially took up the duties of the abbacy again. 'How can he bear it?'

Brother Francis shrugged his shoulders. 'It is for him as it would be for you or me, Tom. He probably thinks he can't bear it, but what else can he do?'

One of the first and worst hurdles for Father Peregrine coming back among the brethren again was presiding over the community chapter meeting, held in the morning every day in the chapter house after Mass, when a chapter of St Benedict's Rule was read, and the abbot gave an address to the brothers, and the affairs of the community were discussed. Easter Day had fallen early, on the twenty-sixth of March that year, and it was on the thirtieth day of April that Abbot Peregrine took his place for the first time in the chapter house again, to preside over the meeting of the brethren.

The reader that morning was Brother Giles, assistant to Brother Walafrid the herbalist, and he read in his broad Yorkshire accent chapter seventy-two of the Rule, the chapter set for that day.

'Just as there is an evil zeal of bitterness which separates from God and leads to hell, so there is a good zeal which separates from evil and leads to God and life everlasting,' he began, confidently. 'Let monks, therefore, exercise this zeal with the most fervent love. Let them, that is, give one another precedence. Let them bear ...' Brother Giles' voice faltered, and he flushed with embarrassment. 'Let them bear with the greatest patience one another's infirmities —' he gulped, and hurried on, 'whether of body or character. Let them vie in paying obedience one to another. Let none follow what seems good for himself, but rather what is good for another. Let them practise fraternal charity with a pure love. Let them fear God. Let them ... let ... let ... let them love their abbot with a sincere and humble affection.'

Brother Giles cleared his throat and finished hastily, 'Let them prefer nothing whatever to Christ. And may he bring us all alike to life everlasting.' He sat down in confusion.

Abbot Peregrine sat with head bowed, dreading their gaze on him. Then he lifted his face, with the stark, hungry bones, the savage scar and missing teeth and dark, hollow eyes. 'The sacred text in this morning's chapter is from St Paul's letter to the Romans,' he said, "Give one another precedence". That is to say, treat one another with the deepest respect. . . .' He himself hardly knew what he was saying, but he managed to speak to them calmly and lucidly for ten minutes and conduct the business of the meeting. The first hurdle was past.

The next thing to face was his pastoral work with the brothers. Peregrine was worried about his novices. Although he trusted his novice master to guide and discipline them, he knew they needed the opportunity to talk things over with their abbot, too. They had had to make shift without it long enough.

Brother Thomas was asked that morning after chapter to come to the abbot's lodging for his routine conference, to review his progress and consider his vocation. It was the first conversation Brother Tom had had alone with his abbot since the night before he had made his novitiate vows two weeks before Easter, and he found it hard to conceal his shock at the change in Father Peregrine. Those dark, penetrating eyes had never looked at him like that before; not with remote amusement, nor yet probing and challenging, but with . . . Brother Thomas searched for a word, and could only come up with . . . 'gentleness'. The abbot was still straight and authoritative in his bearing, still shrewd in his appraising look, still very much in charge: but the look of him was quite different.

'Grief,' Brother Tom thought. 'It's grief. The man's full of it.' Father Peregrine had been asking him a question, but he had not been listening, and now he blurted out, 'Father, I was there, the night they found you. I can't forget it. I'm so sorry, Father—about your hands. I don't know how you can bear it. Is there any way I can help?'

The abbot looked at him for a moment without speaking, and Brother Tom felt uncomfortable, and wished he had had the sense to keep quiet.

'Thank you for your concern, my son,' said Father Peregrine, evenly. 'You might remember me in your prayers. Sometimes—there are times when I hardly know how to bear it myself. But that is not what we were discussing. I asked you, if you recall, whether things are going well for you, or if you have any difficulty.'

As Brother Tom's father had predicted, the monastic life did not come easily to him. The worst of it was the food; not that the food was bad, but oh, so little of it!

Father Peregrine listened with sympathy to Brother Tom's small and natural difficulties. He liked this straightforward young man, liked his zest for life and his candid way of speaking. It steadied him to concentrate on something other than the horrors that haunted his memory and the nightmare of his helplessness.

When their conversation was finished and Brother Tom left, Father Peregrine sat thinking about him for a moment. 'That young man could save my sanity still,' he said to himself. 'Everything that is whole and healthy and good is there in him.'

Brother Tom, on the other hand, felt unhappy. Leaving the abbot's house, he had a sudden memory of his mother carrying a full basin of milk to the dairy, full almost to the brim, moving with infinite steadiness and care lest she slop it over.

'That's it,' he thought, 'he's like that. He's so full of grief that he daren't relax in case it overflows. He's the abbot. He's all on his own. Oh, God help him, poor soul.'

Brother Tom thought about it through the midday office of Sext and through the midday meal. After the meal, as he was leaving the refectory on his way to work in the vegetable garden, he was still thinking about it when he was hailed by Brother Cyprian, the porter.

'Brother! I've some letters in t' lodge for Father Abbot. I'd thank thee if tha'd spare my old bones and fetch them over to him. Will tha do it for me?'

'Gladly, Brother,' said Tom cheerfully, and walked back to the porter's lodge with old Brother Cyprian, suiting his steps to the old man's slow pace. At the porter's lodge, he stayed talking an hour or more with Brother Cyprian, who had an inexhaustible fund of stories about monks past and present, and seemed to know the history of every brother in the abbey. He was careful in his talk, giving away nothing that could embarrass or damage, but that still left him plenty. Blithely indifferent to the passing of time and to the rule forbidding unnecessary conversation, he would have gone on all afternoon, but eventually Tom's conscience could no longer ignore the fact that he was at this moment supposed to be working in the vegetable garden, and he picked up the abbot's letters and stood up to go.

'Aye, good lad, thanks for that. Th'art going by that way aren't tha?'

'I am,' said Tom, with a smile. He was now. He'd been going in the opposite direction in the first place. He took the letters, bade farewell to Brother Cyprian and strolled back across the courtyard, through the refectory and across the cloister to the abbot's house. He hesitated a moment, but the door was ajar, and he knocked shyly, then pushed it open and stepped inside.

Across the room, Father Peregrine was seated at his table, evidently engaged in study, for he had an untidy pile of manuscripts spread on the great oak table in front of him. He was not looking at them, though, nor did he see Brother Tom come in. He was sitting hunched over his table, gazing dully at nothing in particular, sitting very still, except that he was repeating one slow gesture. He was wiping the side of his scarred hand slowly across his mouth, like a little child that wipes away the crumbs of food before he runs out to play, or the old man whose frail and shaky hand wipes away the dribble of saliva from the sunken lips of his toothless mouth.

It could have been absentmindedness, could have been the unconscious gesture of a man deep in thought. But watching, Tom realised (and the realisation wrung him) that the slow, repeated movement, the slight frown, the gazing but unseeing eyes—all were nothing to do with being lost in thought or absent dreaming. The man was tortured by unbearable misery; at last he let his hand drop, and laid his face down upon it, not weeping, hardly even breathing, just tensely, despairingly still.

Brother Tom felt ashamed that his response was a strange, unreasonable resentment. His discomfort crystallised into a prayer, 'Oh God, what do I do now?'

He felt awkward about being there, witnessing the misery that lay behind his abbot's dignified and un-ruffled composure. He wanted to slip away but could not ignore the question that whispered inside: 'If it was me? If it was me—could I face it alone?' And yet he was afraid to intrude. As quietly as he could, he stole across the room, put the letters down on the pile of books, and sat down on the stool that stood before the table, facing the motionless man. He waited a moment, leaned his elbow on the table, leaned his chin on his hand. He wanted to touch him, but dared not; wanted to help him weep, but had no idea how to.

In the end, though, he could no longer concentrate on his own apprehension and self-consciousness. Instinct got the better of him, and reaching out his hand he laid it on the other man's arm without even thinking.

Father Peregrine lifted his head and looked at him. For a minute, his eyes were bewildered, unfocused in the scarred and haggard face. His lips worked a little, but no sound emerged, like a man who has forgotten how to speak.

Then, with a sigh, he smiled, and looked with attention at Brother Tom. 'I do beg your pardon, Brother,' he said quietly, in a most normal, level tone, 'I was not aware of you. Can I help?'

Tom was dumbfounded.

'I doubt it,' he said at last, bluntly. 'Not in the state you're in.'

Father Peregrine just looked at him, opened his mouth to speak, but closed it again, shook his head, shrugged his shoulders and said nothing.

Again the picture flashed in Tom's mind of his mother carrying the bowl of milk, carefully, oh so carefully. 'One jog and he'll spill the lot,' he thought, 'and by my faith he needs to spill that grief.'

'Maybe, if you could tell me, Father ... well, perhaps I could help?' ventured Tom, unsure, feeling irritated at his own uneasiness in the face of the desolation his superior was struggling to master.

'Son, it is good of you to ask,' he said eventually. 'But my burdens are not for you to carry.' His voice was a little uneven, and the tension of maintaining his self-control was causing him to shake slightly.'My son, forgive my discourtesy. Unless your errand is urgent, might we discuss it some other time?'

Half of Brother Tom wanted to say, 'Of course, Father, I quite understand,' and beat a hasty retreat. He never knew where the other half got the courage from, but he replied, 'To be honest with you, I've forgotten why I came. But I know why I'm not going.'

Without giving himself time to think better of it, he followed his impulse, and leaping to his feet dragged the heavy table askew so that he could approach his abbot—who watched him, wide-eyed, white-faced and, Tom realised with a stab of pity, scared. Brother Tom seized the stool, placed it emphatically beside his superior's chair, and sitting on it, took the man in his arms and held him close. 'It's all right,' he said gently, 'you can let it go.' He cursed himself for a fool as he felt the awful rigidity of him, like a man of wood; but he persisted, holding him, not speaking, his thoughts racing. 'Oh well, might as well be hung for a sheep as for a lamb. Faith, I wish I'd shut the door. I hope to God nobody walks in on this. Maybe I should go now. ...'

But as Brother Tom held him and the fortress of his iron self-control was replaced at last, at last, by the fortress of the arms of someone who loved him more than went in awe of him, Peregrine began to weep, and wept until he lost all self-control and abandoned himself to sobbing grief. 'My hands ...' he wept, the words barely intelligible, 'Oh, God, how shall I bear the loss of my hands? To have died would have been nothing ... oh, but my hands ... oh ... oh God. ...' and the words were lost in uncontrollable tears.

What comfort could Brother Tom bring but his presence and his silence and his arms holding him?

The bell for None began to ring, and the monotony of the bell's clang, which normally spoke peace to Tom, suddenly infuriated him. The Office? What insane futility! When a man has lost his skills, his independence and all his sense of dignity, must the afternoon Office intrude on his grieving?

But Peregrine lifted himself away from Tom's embrace, and sat for a moment, shaken, his breath coming unsteadily still. He dug in his pocket for his handkerchief, and shakily wiped his eyes and blew his nose. 'Unless I am mistaken, my son, that is the bell for None. My lateness may reasonably be excused without explanation, but I doubt if yours will. Perhaps you would spare me that disclosure and be there in good time.'

That was the nearest he would stoop to begging Tom not to tell anyone, but Tom understood well enough, and he never did tell anyone until after Peregrine's death.

Brother Tom nodded soberly and, replacing his stool, dragged the table back into position.

'Brother Thomas.' The abbot's quiet voice arrested

him as he reached the door. 'Thank you. From my
heart, Brother, thank you.'

This small incident remained a living bond between
the two men ever afterward, and kindled in Brother
Tom a deep protective love for his abbot. As for the rest
of the brothers, Father Peregrine bore their curious
glances without a word, and their pity too, and knew
very well their doubts as to his fitness to rule them any
longer.

In the end, though, it became apparent to all the
community that he had a new authority about him now.
For whereas before he had ruled with a natural strength
and ability over other men, now he was learning to cling
to the grace of God and find his strength there. He had
commanded their respect before, and it had been based
on the fear of his power over them. He earned their
respect in a new way now, respect mingled with admiration and love, because he had found out for himself
what it was to be weak—weak enough to need his
brothers' help—and his authority over them now was
born of humble understanding.

Great-uncle Edward had many tales to tell of Father
Peregrine, after the terrible thing that happened to him.
Uncle Edward said it crippled his body, but it set his
spirit free. He said that most men would have become
bitter and closed in, but Peregrine did not. He used his
own weakness as a bridge to cross over to his brothers,
when they too were weak. Having lost everything, he
gave his weakness to God, and it became his strength.

In a way, all the tales are one tale, the tale of how
God's power is found in weakness. But that is the story
of the whole of life, if you know how to read it right.

Mother sat for a while in silence. The candle had burned
low, and the room was very quiet.

'Are you asleep, Melissa?' she said then.

'No. I was thinking about Tom. He was brave, wasn't
he?'

'Mmm, yes. Yes, he couldn't be sure how it would turn out.'

'And his name—Father Columba, I mean. He did get gentle, like a dove.'

'Yes, it was a good name after all. Everyone still called him Father Peregrine, though, and he could still be pretty fierce and tough, when he needed to be. The difference was, now they weren't too scared to call him it to his face.'

Mother said in the morning she was sorry she ever started to tell me about Abbot Peregrine, because that night I woke the whole family, screaming and struggling in my sleep, terrified by nightmares of those grim vengeful thugs, stamping with indifferent cruelty on the fine, scholarly hands, flung out in helplessness on the stone chapel floor.

III
HUMBLE PIE

It was one of those hot, stifling days in late June, and the classroom was stuffy. One lazy fly buzzed monotonously, occasionally colliding with the windowpane. I looked at the fly, and at the window, and my gaze was drawn outside to the school buildings and the field beyond, where there was a row of poplar trees, graceful and slender, their topmost branches stirring even on that still day.

The teacher was writing on the blackboard, the chalk stabbing and scraping industriously. 'Tenir', she wrote, and 'Venir'. She underlined them heavily, and pushed her glasses more firmly onto the bridge of her nose as she fixed us with her severe glance.

'The compounds of *tenir* and *venir* form the past historic similarly. The same applies of course to *retenir, revenir,* and so on.' She whipped round again and attacked the blackboard with the chalk once more, writing *'je tins, tu tins, il tint ...'*

I could see the sickroom through the window, across the tennis court. I had been in there twice. It was white and bare with a calendar on the wall, and a picture of the Queen Mother. I tried to imagine the infirmary at the monastery of St Alcuin. Perhaps its walls were built of big blocks of honey-coloured stone. The rooms would be smaller than elsewhere in the abbey, to allow for a sick man to lie alone in peace ... in peace or in pain and fear. But Great-uncle Edward had not left Peregrine alone with his pain and his fear. He had understood, and stayed with him, talking to him gently, helping him through the worst of the horror. And then Brother Tom, greatly daring, giving him a safe place to cry. I found it easy, in my mind, to wander in the infirmary, to see the brothers bending over the sick man, caring for him: but the other ... I felt a strange shyness as I imagined that reserved, solitary man, racked with his grief, in the arms of the young brother. It seemed too intimate, too raw a thing even to think about, as though I should glimpse it with reverence, then tiptoe away ...

'Melissa, did you hear me? Are you listening at all?'

I looked, bewildered, at the teacher, my mouth slightly ajar, and struggled to adjust my blank expression to something more intelligent-looking. She took off her glasses, the better to glare at me.

'*Vint à passer,*' snapped Mrs Kerr. '*Un facteur vint à passer.*' *Vint?* I looked at the blackboard. From *venir. Un facteur?* What the dickens was that? *Un facteur* came to pass. Crumbs.

'I beg your pardon, Mrs Kerr, I can't remember what *un facteur* means.'

'*Un facteur,*' said Mrs Kerr, her black eyes glittering at me like little jet beads, 'is a postman.'

A postman. A postman came to pass. 'Please, God,' I begged, silently. I could feel the palms of my hands sweating. 'I don't know,' I said helplessly, at last.

'Melissa, you have not been paying the slightest attention to this lesson. I have just explained at some length, that when followed by an infinitive, the verb *venir à* takes the meaning "happen to". *Un facteur vint à passer* uses the past historic of *venir à,* and demonstrates this use of the verb. It means "a postman happened to pass". Now that I have explained to you what we were all concentrating on perhaps you would like to tell us what you were thinking about?'

'I ... I was imagining the infirmary, in a monastery long ago ... what it would be like,' I mumbled.

Mrs Kerr was waiting. She seemed to expect something more of me. 'It was a story,' I explained, 'about a monk who was terribly hurt and crying and the other monk loved him and comforted him.' I couldn't think of anything else to say.

She looked at me with her little black eyes. Like currants looking out of a bun, I thought.

'You must learn to apply your mind to the subject before you, Melissa. You will not learn by dreaming, or by reading sentimental novels. You will learn only if you work.' She settled her glasses back on her nose and seized the text book.

'Turn to page 131 please, girls. I want you to look at section B, which deals with the omission of the definite article in the expression *plus ... plus ...*; the more, the more as in *Plus je travaille, plus j'apprends.*'

I looked at the teacher, then down at my book. The page in front of me was full of words, but empty of meaning. Sentimental? Is that what sentimental is? When for once, instead of looking the other way, someone dares to stretch out a timid hand to comfort and to heal? I thought about Mother. She didn't seem a sentimental person. Tough as old boots, Daddy said: but she had told me the story. With that same feeling of shyness, I approached the picture in my mind again ... the heat and indignity of giving yourself up to sobbing in someone's arms, someone you didn't know very well, with your nose running and your face bathed in sweat and tears, trusting because you had to, because you couldn't carry it alone any more. ... Is it sentimental to speak about that sort of thing? Was Mrs Kerr right? I looked up at her pale, tight-lipped face and considered her rigid, ramrod-straight, thin body, buttoned up to the neck in a suit of hard, grey fabric. Perhaps it was Mrs Kerr who ... maybe no one ever ... did she sometimes—like me—bury her face in the pillow at night and cry for sheer sadness at the loneliness of it all?

'Melissa!' thundered Mrs Kerr.

By the grace and mercy of God, the bell rang.

As soon as the school day ended, I ran like the wind up the hill to the gates of the county primary school where Mary and Beth went to school. Although their day finished ten minutes before ours, the two schools were so close that if I ran, I would be in time to find Mother and Cecily, waiting at the top of the hill with the other mothers.

Halfway up the hill, I paused and shaded my eyes with my hand against the low afternoon sun. Yes, she was still there, with Cecily and Mary and Beth milling around her. She was listening to their urgent chatter. I ran up to the top, dodging through the last straggle of mothers and children coming away from the gates.

'Hello, Cecily!' I shouted. She ran to me, and I scooped her up in my arms. Her belligerent little face dimpled with delight, and she patted my face with her grubby fingers.

'Had a good day?' asked Mother, as we set off slowly homewards.

'No. Awful,' I said. 'I couldn't concentrate on anything. I've been in trouble all day. What's for tea?'

'Baked potatoes and cheese,' said Mother. 'Why couldn't you concentrate?'

'I was trying to imagine Father Peregrine, and the infirmary, and Brother Tom. I was trying to picture them in my mind.'

'Mummy we've learned a new song!' said Beth. 'It's about water, and I can do all the first bit. Listen!'

She launched into her song, and then Cecily wanted us to listen to her sing a song, too, and then Therese overtook us as we turned in at the gate.

Therese was sixteen, pink, and plump and gentle, with her fall of brown hair like Mother's, but light blue eyes full of laughter like Daddy's. She went into the kitchen and put the kettle on.

Home, I was home. The smell of it, the peace of it! Although it was so small, and we were so many, somehow our house was like a bowl of quietness and light. As I crossed its threshold, I relaxed with a huge sigh, and the world of school dropped from me like a cloak.

The kitchen was filled with a wonderful aroma of baked potato. Therese pushed a mug of tea into my hand as I came in. Home. It closed about me like wings folding around me. Therese gave me a thick slice of bread and jam. I sat down at the kitchen table, utterly content.

'In trouble all day, you said?' Mother's voice broke in on my contentment, as she came into the kitchen. 'Thank you, Therese,' she said as she took her cup of tea. 'And nightmares last night. I think we'll have to have a different story tonight.'

'Mother, no!' I protested. 'You don't mean it? I will concentrate at school, I promise. I've been waiting all day for the story!'

'I think, maybe,' said Mother slowly, 'once you know more about Father Peregrine, you might actually work better at school. You certainly won't have any more nightmares. But listen, my dove, if I find your work suffers as a result of these stories, then no more. You must learn to keep your imagination separate, a walled garden with a little green door to go in by. Go in through the door in your lunch hour and in the evening, but when it's lesson time, you come out of the garden and you shut the door and turn your back on it. Understood?'

'Mother, I promise,' I said.

After tea, Daddy came home, and played the piano and sang to us until bath-time. Then he retreated behind a book with a mug of beer and a cheese sandwich while Therese and I got out our homework. In my mind I closed the little green door firmly, and worked single-mindedly on my maths homework for half an hour. As the little procession of clean, pink children came out of the bathroom, I slammed the book shut. 'Finished! And nothing else to do!'

The little ones went in to kiss Daddy goodnight, and then I followed them upstairs to the bedroom. They had to have their prayers first, and their game. Mary and Beth sat down on their beds while Mother drew the curtains and lit the candle. They prayed the Lord's Prayer, and Mother blessed them, and then it was time for the game.

'What does the elephant say?' asked Mother.

'Triumph! Triumph!' they shouted, brandishing their arms as trunks and stamping around the bedroom.

'And what is the only thing an elephant is afraid of?' she said.

'A mousie!' they cried, all together.

'And what does the mousie say?'

'Weakness! Weakness! Weakness!' they squeaked, scrabbling about with tiny steps and twitching noses, their hands gathered up like little claws. It was Cecily's game really, but Mary and Beth loved to join in.

'So who is the stronger, the elephant or the mousie?' Mother asked.

'The mousie!' they shouted again.

'And the elephant trumpets triumph, but the mousie says—'

'Weakness! Weakness! Weakness!' until they fell about laughing. Nearly every night they played this game. Mother said they needed to learn while they were still young that the two words belonged together.

'Go on with the story, Mother!' I begged; but she would not, not until the last elephant had trumpeted its triumph and the last mouse had pleaded its weakness and lay quiet in its bed.

Then Mother sat for a moment in her chair, little Cecily curled up on her lap with her head cradled in the crook of Mother's arm.

Beth yawned a huge yawn.

'Very well,' said Mother, 'your story. There was a story that became a legend in the abbey of St Alcuin; and Uncle Edward's great-niece, to whom these stories were first told, never tired of hearing this story, which came to be known as "Humble Pie".'

Father Matthew, the novice master, was notorious for his strictness. All the little faults and misdemeanours that most men would have turned a blind eye to, he pounced on like a cat on a mouse, and kept strict discipline and expected high standards among the novices in his charge. Brother Michael had just recently made his solemn vows, leaving in the novitiate Brother Francis, Brother Thomas, Brother Theodore, Brother Cormac and Brother Thaddeus. Of them all it was Brother Theodore who was most often in disgrace, but it should really have been Brother Thomas and Brother Francis, because they were always getting into scrapes and were inclined towards practical jokes and light, foolish conversation. Father Matthew had twice that week found them helpless with laughter over some silly tale, and had set them to tasks which kept them occupied at opposite ends of the abbey, in the hope of calming them down a bit.

Now this Brother Thomas, the same who had held the abbot in his arms and comforted his grief, was a big lad and everlastingly hungry. Sleepless with hunger one night, he had crept out of the dormitory, stolen down to the kitchen, and spirited away from the larder an apple pie, which he devoured with great speed, sitting on the stairs. He licked every crumb from his fingers, sighed happily, and crept back to his bed undetected. Tom did not believe he would ever get used to the meagre provision of a monastery table. The stories handed down to us paint a picture of monks eating and drinking like gluttons, but it was not true in that abbey, at any rate. Even the cook was thin and sour—but more of him later.

Brother Tom told Brother Francis about it as they ate their hunk of bread after morning Office, which turned out to be a foolish indiscretion, because Brother Francis told Brother Thaddeus during the time set aside for private reading and meditation after breakfast. He was unfortunately overheard by Father Matthew, who rebuked him for indulging in idle gossip and assured him this would not be the end of it.

Brother Thaddeus, on the way out of Terce, the mid-morning Office, warned Brother Tom that Father Matthew had been apprised of his misdoings, and like most men with a guilty conscience, Tom looked round for someone else to blame.

The monastic life is hard enough, you would think, but in those days it was dreadful! Discipline was strict, especially under the likes of Father Matthew! Every little fault or sin or accident was taken seriously, and must be confessed to teach the monk humility. It was not enough, either, just to say 'Sorry!' as you or I might. Not likely! The Rule of St Benedict, which was the rule by which the Benedictine monks lived, stipulated that any brother who had to be corrected for a fault, or who was in trouble with his superior had to prostrate himself on the ground at his superior's feet, and stay there until he blessed him and gave him permission to get up.

Father Gregory, the previous abbot, while agreeing with the principles that lay behind this practice, nevertheless saw that it could create problems, he himself having once tripped over the feet of a prostrate brother in passing. He therefore modified the rule slightly, and in his abbey, the practice was that any of the brothers who committed a fault, or otherwise gave offence, should kneel before the one he had offended, saying, 'I humbly confess my fault of speaking during the Great Silence' (or whatever it was he'd done wrong), 'and I ask forgiveness of you, my brother, and of God.' Father Gregory was quite firm that the offended party should not hang about, keeping the miscreant on his knees, but should respond at once, 'God forgives you, Brother, and so do I,' which blessing would be the end of the matter, and life could go on as normal. This seemed a humiliating, almost unbearable procedure to the young men who were new to monastic life, and it wasn't supposed to be easy, but it was a quick way to learn to be humble!

But worst of all, anyone who had done something wrong was supposed to kneel before the whole community and confess it, either before lunch when the brothers had said grace, or at the beginning of community chapter, before the reading of the Rule and the abbot's talk. Poor Brother Tom knew well enough that Father Matthew would have him on his knees before the whole community, confessing to sneaking a pie at midnight, and he was after Brother Francis' blood for giving him away.

At this hour of the day, which was about ten o'clock in the morning, the brothers were supposed to be about their daily tasks, but instead of heading for the vegetable garden, which was his present place of work, Brother Tom set off hastily to intercept Brother Francis on his way to the scriptorium, where the books for the library were copied and the illuminated manuscripts were painted. The work Brother Francis turned out was nothing special, but it was reasonably accurate, and it kept him away from Brother Tom, or at least it was supposed to.

Tom saw him on his way there, and the sight of Francis, walking slowly and peacefully along the deserted cloister with the air of a man who hadn't a care in the world, enraged him still further. Tom overtook him, grabbed him by the shoulder, and swung him round to face him with his back against the wall, in one violent movement.

'What have you done, you stupid blabbermouth?' he hissed. He would rather have roared like a mad bull, but his sense of self-preservation restrained him; he was in enough trouble already. He contented himself with glaring at Francis and demanding, 'Now what am I supposed to do?'

Francis' coolness was as much a habit with him as his black tunic, and he regarded Tom calmly, apparently unmoved by his red face and the quivers of rage that shook him. His eyes flickered momentarily, but he spoke with what struck Tom as heartless indifference: 'Do?' he said, 'Well, I suppose you'll have to confess it at chapter tomorrow morning.'

Tom could have hit him. He glared at him, speechless for a moment, and then spluttered, 'Fine friend you are, you big-mouthed toad! You don't care a bit, do you!'

Francis did actually care, but chose to pretend he didn't. That was the way with him. The more he cared, the more indifferent he pretended to be. The guilt and embarrassment that filled him because he had unwittingly betrayed his friend to Father Matthew he now concealed beneath a tone of defensive irritation. 'Well, it's your own fault, Brother! You shouldn't have done it. You didn't ask me to keep it a secret, did you?'

Tom launched into an indignant reply, ignoring Francis' sudden gesture intended to silence him, and warning, 'Ssh!'

'Don't "shush" me, man! I haven't ...'

'Shut *up*, Tom,' muttered Brother Francis. 'Father Abbot ...'

In spite of his distinctive gait, they had neither of them heard Father Peregrine before he saw them, and they stood helplessly as he approached. He looked at them, eyebrows raised in surprise. 'What is your dispute, brothers?'

Tom stared at him, dumbly. Francis, after a quick glance at his friend, spoke first. 'He ... I ... Father Matthew ...' he began, and then tailed off into silence, not wishing to be guilty of betraying his friend to the abbot, as well as the novice master.

This simple speech put Father Peregrine in the picture fairly well, but he thought he might as well have the details. 'Yes?' he said, looking from one to the other of them.

So poor Brother Tom had to tell what had happened, and wretchedly mumbled the whole story with downcast eyes, ending by explaining how Father Matthew had overheard it all as Brother Francis related the tale to Brother Thaddeus.

'Well, it was your own fault!' Francis burst out. 'If you lived for more than your belly you wouldn't be in this predicament.'

Tom's head shot up, and he opened his mouth to reply, but Father Peregrine silenced him. 'Enough of that,' he said. 'Brother Francis,' he continued calmly, 'it is my opinion that you owe Brother Thomas an apology for your rudeness and self-righteousness, as well as for gossiping about him. One man's sin is not an appropriate topic for another man's conversation.'

Francis looked at him for a moment and met that direct, fierce, hawk's eye, and without a word got down on to his knees before Brother Tom.

'I confess ...' he said, 'I humbly confess my rudeness and self-righteousness, and my careless gossip, and I ask forgiveness, Brother, of you and of God.'

Tom couldn't bear this. He felt as though he was being choked. 'Oh, no, get up. Please!' he said, but Father Peregrine said, 'He has asked your forgiveness, Brother. Will you dismiss him so ungraciously?'

Tom had always found the experience of kneeling to ask forgiveness appalling. It had never occurred to him until this moment that it could be just as hard to forgive. The Rule made it clear that humble, heart-felt forgiveness was what was required, not just the form of words. For a moment, the thought of Father Matthew flashed through Brother Tom's mind again, as well as the prospect of kneeling before the community to confess his fault at community chapter, and he wasn't at all sure he forgave Brother Francis.

Francis, who could read his friend like a book, knew

the struggle going on inside him. He felt desperately ashamed of himself. 'I really am sorry, Tom,' he said in a small voice, and looked up into his face with the disguise of indifference torn away.

Tom's heart went out to his friend. 'God forgives you, and so do I!' he said heartily, and Francis got thankfully to his feet. They looked at Father Peregrine, unsure whether they were free to go or not, and he smiled at them imperturbably.

'Now you, Brother Thomas, should go and find the cook, and confess your fault to him and ask his pardon.'

Brother Tom's jaw dropped. If there could be anything worse than confessing his sin before the community in the chapter meeting, this had to be it. The kitchen was possibly the busiest place in the abbey. Lay servants worked there, as well as two of the brothers, all presided over by Brother Andrew, a sour and irritable Scot, notorious for his impatient and sarcastic tongue. A monk would have the graciousness to pretend not to notice one of his brothers kneeling to a superior to confess a fault, but not the lay servants from the village. They regarded it as good entertainment.

'But ...' began the luckless Tom, then caught the abbot's eye and thought better of it.

His last hopes were dashed as Father Peregrine smiled at him and said, 'You can come and tell me what Brother Andrew says.'

There was no deferring until it was conveniently forgotten, then, or at least until after chapter in the morning, when Brother Andrew would already have heard his confession before the community. He swallowed hard.

'Yes, Father,' he said, and exchanged one desperate glance with Brother Francis before plodding away reluctantly to the kitchens.

'Thank you, Brother Francis. Don't let me detain you any further,' said Father Peregrine, and Francis took himself off to the scriptorium.

Peregrine then set off in search of Father Matthew and found him crossing the courtyard on his way to the gatehouse, with a bundle of letters for the porter.

'A word with you, Father Matthew,' he said pleasantly, and hesitated. Father Matthew was one of those men who had to be handled with care, for good results. 'I have just seen Brother Thomas and Brother Francis,' he continued carefully. 'They have confessed their faults to me of idle gossip and the theft of a pie, and I have given them their penance.' He wondered briefly if Father Matthew would have considered merely apologising to Brother Tom and apologising to the cook to be worthy of the name 'penance', but then, Father Matthew seemed extraordinarily unaware of what it cost them to do it. 'I do not wish to presume on your authority with the novices, Father Matthew, but I think it should not now be necessary for them to confess their faults at community chapter. I hope you approve of the line of action I have taken,' he said politely, well aware that Father Matthew had no choice but to approve.

'Yes, of course, Father. We will consider the matter closed, then?'

'I think so, Father,' said Peregrine. 'Thank you, that's all.'

Brother Tom found Brother Andrew in the frantically busy hour before lunch. Brother Andrew was vaguely aware of him as an obstacle in the congested pathways of his kitchen but took no notice of him for a moment, then nearly walked into him on his way back to the pantry with a huge cheese in his hands.

'Whatever is it you want, Brother?' he snapped.

Tom looked at him, but felt as if his tongue was stuck to the roof of his mouth, and just stood there clenching and unclenching his fists, as red as a beetroot.

'What in heaven's name ails you, man? Do you want anything or no? Can you not see how busy I am?' roared the old Scot.

'Father Abbot sent me,' whispered Tom huskily.

'Well?' said Brother Andrew, perplexed as well as irritated. 'Here, take this to the pantry; mind you wrap it well,' he said to a passing servant, handing over the cheese.

Tom fell to his knees before him, his hands clenched into fists, unable to look up. The old man's face softened, and a glimmer of amusement came into his eyes. He had noticed the absence of the pie as he went into the pantry this morning, and he guessed what this was all about. The bustle of the kitchen ceased as several pairs of curious eyes and ears gave their full attention to the scene.

'Brother, I humbly confess my fault. I ... I came down here last night and stole a pie from the pantry and I ... ask forgiveness of you and of God.'

Tom thought it was probably the worst moment of his life. The kitchen was utterly quiet. He felt a bony hand on his shoulder, and looked up into old Brother Andrew's eyes which were dancing with merriment.

'Brother, I esteem your courage,' he said. 'God forgives you, and so do I. Father Abbot is a very hard man.'

Tom got to his feet without a word, and stumbled out of the kitchen. Once through the door, he stood still, and took a deep breath. For the first time since eating the wretched pie, his heart felt as light as a bird. It was over.

He set off cheerfully for the vegetable garden, and turning the corner almost collided with Father Peregrine.

'I did it,' he said, exultantly.

'Did you? Well done. Let that be finished with, then, you need not confess your fault to the community,' said Peregrine, then stood there, eyeing Tom thoughtfully for a moment, as if there was something more he wanted to say. 'I was looking for you,' he said. 'What did Brother Andrew say?'

'He said he esteemed my courage,' said Tom shyly, 'and he forgave me.' He grinned at Father Peregrine. 'And he said Father Abbot is a very hard man!'

Peregrine continued to look at him thoughtfully, and Tom was just beginning to wonder if he'd said the wrong thing, when slowly, awkwardly, Peregrine knelt before him.

Tom was horrified. He knew it hurt badly for the abbot to bend that crippled leg and kneel—he didn't even kneel during the Office—and besides that, he was covered with embarrassment, anxious lest anyone should come round the corner and see his lord abbot kneeling before him.

'I humbly confess my fault, Brother,' said Father Peregrine. 'When I was a novice, twenty-five years ago, I, too, was hungry in the night, and, like you, I crept down to the kitchen, and I stole three pies, and I ate the lot. I was never found out, and to this day I've never owned up to anyone. I ask your forgiveness and God's for placing on your shoulders a burden I myself was unwilling to bear.'

Tom was utterly astonished. He could not even imagine this man as a novice, hungry, struggling with temptation and failing. All he wanted to say was, 'Oh, for heaven's sake, get *up*,' but he knew that was not what was required of him.

'God forgives you, and I forgive you, Father,' he said. 'Oh, please get up!' and he helped Father Peregrine to his feet again.

That was not the end of the story, though. That evening, in the hour before Compline when the novices had gathered in their community room in the novitiate to relax and converse, there was a knock on the door.

Opening it, Brother Cormac was confronted with Brother Michael, Brother Andrew's assistant in the kitchen, smiling at him and carrying a tray laden with pies, one for each of them, steaming and fragrant and delicious.

'Father Abbot sends these with his compliments,' he said. 'He asks me to say that he thought the novices might be hungry. Also he bids me tell you, the recipe is his own, and it is called Humble Pie. He says he has tasted some himself, today, and he finds it very nourishing.'

The candle guttered, and went out. It had burnt to the end. 'Goodnight,' whispered Mother. 'Come down for a hot drink, Melissa, if you want one,' and after laying the sleeping Cecily in her bed, and tucking the covers round her, she tiptoed out of the room.

IV
CLARE DE MONTANY

My eyes opened, and I lay still. All was quiet. I raised myself on one elbow. Mary and Beth had crept out of bed and gone to play, but Therese was still asleep, buried deep under her covers. Cecily was still asleep too, curled up with her cheek pillowed on her hand, her long, dark eyelashes resting on her soft pink cheek.

Cecily looked delightful when she was asleep. Her mouth was like a little rosebud, and her curls spread on the pillow. She was a picture of vulnerable innocence. No one could have guessed, looking at her now, what utter weariness my parents' faces wore after a morning of Cecily's company. Daddy said she was like a natural disaster, a mysterious act of God which we could only suffer patiently and pray for strength to endure. She was only two, but Mother said she felt as though she'd aged more in those two years than in all the other thirty-eight years of her life put together. From the moment those great, china-blue eyes opened in the morning, Cecily was in conflict with the world, fighting her way forward with a dauntless spirit, a will of iron and an ear-splitting voice.

I lay down again cautiously. I did not want to wake her up. Today was Sunday, nearly the best part of the week. The best part was waking up on Saturday morning to the realisation that the whole weekend lay before me.

No school for two whole days. *Freedom.* But Sunday was quite good: half the weekend left, anyway. Any minute now the house would erupt into chaos as Daddy tried to get everyone ready for church, tried to find the little ones' socks and cardigans, tried to convince Mother that ten more minutes in bed was ten minutes too long, and finally lost his temper with everyone.

It was the same every Sunday. Our family would arrive at church, still slightly breathless, Mother looking deceptively serene and composed as she swept up the aisle in her voluminous skirt, finding the first hymn for the little ones just in time to sing the last verse. Nobody could have imagined, to look at her, the terrible virago of twenty minutes ago, whose eyes flashed fire and whose tongue lashed us all, who had snatched up a bellowing Cecily, slapped her hard, and dumped her unceremoniously into the car.

It was the same this Sunday. Mother took our hymnbooks from the sidesman at the door, flashing him her radiant and disarming smile, and then sailed up the aisle to our pew, with us children trailing behind her, and Daddy bringing up the rear with Cecily clinging round his neck, still hiccupping and sniffing, her tragic face peeping over his shoulder.

It is a curious thing how an hour in the swimming pool, or an hour in the theatre, is gone in five minutes, whereas an hour in church on a Sunday morning seems to drag on for eternity. The worst part of all was always Father Bennett's sermon. Never in the history of mankind had one man been able to make fifteen minutes seem so long, of that I was sure. Daddy said the trouble was he had nothing to say, but he loved saying it.

He stood up now in the pulpit and closed his eyes. Daddy gave Cecily a jelly-baby and a book about farm animals to keep her quiet.

'May the words of my mouth and the meditation of my heart be always acceptable in thy sight,' boomed Father Bennett, 'O Lord, my Redeemer and my Rock.'

He opened his eyes, and gripping the edge of the pulpit, looked down on us. "Simon, son of Jonah," he announced, taking his text from the reading we had just heard, "you are a happy man." He allowed his gaze to sweep slowly round the congregation. 'And why was he a happy man? *Not* because he was especially rich, because he was *not*. *Not* because he was especially well educated, because he was *not*. *Not* because he was especially important, because he was *not*. Yet our Lord said to him, "Simon, son of Jonah, *you*"' (here he stabbed his index finger forcefully at an imaginary figure standing a few feet in front of him, suspended in mid-air above the heads of the congregation) "—are a happy man."

I glanced at Mother. Her mouth was twitching slightly, but she sat upright in her seat, and her eyes did not waver from the preacher's face. I looked across at Daddy. He was smiling encouragingly at Cecily, slipping her another jelly-baby, a green one because that was her favourite, and silently mouthing 'Moo! Moo!' and 'Baa! Baa!' at her, as she showed him the pictures in her book.

Beth was looking at the pictures in the children's service book, and Mary was watching the little jewel-coloured pools of light that freckled the pew as the morning sunshine streamed through the stained-glass window. Therese was looking at the congregation with her eyes slightly crossed to see if she could see two of everybody.

I sighed. Father Bennett was well launched into his dissertation on the exact source of the happiness of Simon Bar-Jonah. I looked at the war-memorial plaque, with its painted relief of a golden sword stuck through a coiled red dragon, and read through all the names written there. Daddy had told me, when I was only seven, that the list of names referred to all those who had died in the services, and added that I need have no cause for anxiety since they had all been men.

I looked at the flowers, gladioli and carnations and

roses, that stood in front of the pulpit. They were quivering slightly from Father Bennett's emphatic thumps on the pulpit desk. I looked up at him with curiosity. He didn't mind kneeling down in the church service, to confess his sins to God. I tried to picture him kneeling in front of Daddy, saying, 'I humbly confess that I have bored you with tedious sermons, and made God seem very small and far away like looking through the wrong end of the binoculars.' I tried to imagine him kneeling before Stan Birkett, the dustman—a small, weary, disillusioned man—saying, 'I humbly confess that you wanted me to be your friend, but I would only be your vicar. ...' No, it didn't fit. And yet, he didn't mind kneeling down to God. Unless ... perhaps he wasn't sure God was there at all?

Just now he was beaming at his congregation with a confident smile, saying: '... and assuredly, as we confess the divinity and supremacy of our blessed Lord, we too can rejoice in his promise of blessedness, and lay hold of that coveted commendation, "Simon, son of Jonah, *you* are a happy man!" In the name of the Father and of the Son and of the Holy Spirit, Amen; Hymn 452 "Oh Happy band of pilgrims, if onward ye will tread". Hymn 452.'

'We are a happy lot this morning,' murmured Mother cynically, as she picked up her book. The congregation sang boisterously: the hymn following the sermon always had the holiday air of young cows let out to frolic in the grass after a long winter spent cooped up in a barn. We roared the words:

> The trials that beset you,
> The sorrows ye endure,
> The manifold temptations
> That death alone can cure—
> What are they but his jewels
> Of right celestial worth?
> What are they but the ladder,
> Set up to heaven on earth?

Mother looked down at me and smiled. 'Peregrine,' she said softly, and I smiled back; but at the time, I didn't understand what she meant.

Then came the long, long prayers. Pages and pages of them. Cecily never made it through to Communion but always had to be taken out at some point, because she insisted on banging her foot loudly on the pew, or imitating the cries of the seagulls outside. This morning, she was removed halfway through the prayers of inter-cession, hysterical with rage because the last green jelly-baby had gone. If I listened carefully, I could hear Daddy playing 'to market, to market to buy a fat pig' with her, outside in the porch, but I forced myself to concentrate as Father Bennett's voice droned on.

'This is my body, which is given for you,' he intoned. I wrestled with the thought. How could he speak about it like that? What had it to do with us? A man, so long ago, beaten, dirty, exhausted; his face streaked with tears and blood and spit; pinned to a cross with nails through his hands and feet. What had it to do with us? The compelling defencelessness of his courage and his vulnerable love had, so far as I could see, left us unmoved. Father Bennett, whom Daddy described as a fatuous twit, had nothing anywhere about him that reminded me of the struggle and self-abandonment of Jesus. When it came to it, nor did I.

'Draw near with faith ...' boomed Father Bennett, and I got up from my knees and sat waiting until Mother stood up and we all followed her into the Communion queue. Therese had been confirmed two years ago, and I had been confirmed last autumn, but Mary and Beth were too young to receive the bread and wine, and instead Father Bennett laid his hands on their heads and blessed them.

We knelt in a row at the altar rail; first Therese, then Mary, then Mother, then Beth, then me, and I held out my hands to receive the Communion wafer.

'The body of Christ, broken for you,' said Father

Bennett, as he pressed the white, translucent wafer, with the little imprint of a crucifix on it, into my hand.

'Amen,' I said, and as I tried to swallow the dry, tasteless thing before old Father Carnforth got to me with the wine, I asked myself, 'How? How is it the body of Christ? What has happened to his hurting, his smile, his hands, his sore, dusty feet?'

'The blood of Jesus, shed for you,' said Father Carnforth in his aged, asthmatic wheeze, and I took the chalice and sipped the deep red, rich velvety wine. The delicious, intoxicating taste of it spread round my mouth, fiery and sweet. That seemed a bit more like Jesus.

I got to my feet and walked back to our pew, hands folded and eyes downcast, as Mother had taught me. In the silence before the prayers which ended the service, while the rest of the people took Communion, and then Father Bennett consumed the remains of the wine and washed and dried the chalice, I abandoned my questioning and played a whispered game of 'I Spy' with Beth.

At last it was time for the final prayers. I was itching to be out in the sunlight, and feeling light-headed with hunger.

We sang our last hymn with gusto, during which Daddy judged there was enough noise going on for it to be safe to re-admit Cecily, and then it was over.

We all shook hands with Father Bennett and said what a lovely morning it was, as we left, except Cecily who refused even to look at him; and then we went home to a huge dinner of roast lamb and new potatoes and greens, with apple pie and cream to follow.

After lunch, Cecily went up to bed for a rest, and Therese took Mary and Beth out to the park.

'I'll come and help you in a minute!' I called to Daddy. I could hear him beginning to tackle the huge pile of washing-up in the kitchen.

Mother was in the living-room, curled up in the corner of the sofa, sipping her coffee. I sat down beside her.

'Tell me a story,' I begged.

'Oh, goodness,' she said, 'my brain's full of dinner, I can't think!' But she had that faraway, meditative, remembering look on her face, and I waited hopefully.

'About Peregrine?' she said.

'Yes, please!'

She sipped at her coffee again, and then cupped her hands round the rough pottery as she thought.

Then she began her story.

The Benedictine Rule laid down that guests of the abbey, who were to be received with honour and courtesy, especially pilgrims and the poor, should always dine with the abbot. Father Peregrine found this duty particularly trying, because the awkwardness of his hands made it difficult for him to eat in the refined and tidy way such occasions demanded of him. He found the effort of concentrating on preventing his hands from letting him down, while at the same time sustaining an intelligent and witty conversation, extremely tiring. In addition, he had to try to finish his dinner at the same time as his guests finished theirs, so as to avoid a ghastly ten minutes of silence while his fascinated guests watched him struggle with the remains of his food. The mere thought of entertaining guests gave him a head-ache. In the end, he hit upon the plan of going into the kitchens before the meal, where Brother Andrew would give him a plate of food to stave off hunger; then he could be served a minute portion of dinner when he sat to eat with guests of the abbey. This alleviated his difficulties considerably, though he was embarrassed by the way his guests looked with alarm at the pathetic amount of food on his plate, and could later be over-heard by the brothers, commenting on what a holy and self-denying man the abbot was.

It was a day of bitter cold and wind, towards the end of February. It had been raining for nearly a week and the light was weak and grey even at midday, and almost dark by late afternoon, when Father Peregrine was sitting in the infirmary with Brother Edward, who was working on Peregrine's hands with his aromatic oils. It was a good place to be, on a day like this, because the infirmary was one of the few places in the abbey which was always kept warm, and today a brazier of charcoal glowed comfortably in the room where they sat.

Brother Francis was sent to them with word from the porter that a family had arrived at the abbey requesting hospitality and a bed for the night.

'Father Chad has received them, and is seeing to their comfort. He says he will bring them to your lodging to dine after Vespers. It is a lady with her daughter and two sons, all of them between eighteen and twenty-five years of age as I judge, travelling to Iona on pilgrimage for the Easter Feast. Besides these are their servants; a groom and a lady's maid.'

'Thank you, brother. Did you enquire the name of the family?'

'Oh, forgive me, Father. I forgot. Father Chad saw to them straight away, I had no conversation with them.'

Francis left them, and Uncle Edward put away his little vials of essential oils; near the brazier he placed the little bowl which held the remains of the mixture of almond oil and essential oils he had been using, that it might slowly evaporate in the warmth, scenting and disinfecting the room.

'Terrible weather for a party on pilgrimage,' he commented.

'It is indeed. Iona is a long way in this foul rain. Still, they have a night to rest and be refreshed. Join us for dinner, Edward,' said Father Peregrine. 'You have more of a gift for conversation than I.'

'Is that a compliment, Father, or a back-handed insult?'

Peregrine grinned at him. 'As you will,' he answered. 'Now I must go to Brother Andrew and beg some bread, for I shall be fasting more or less if we have guests tonight, and what we ate at midday was nothing to compose poetry about. Thank you for your ministrations,

Brother. My hands ache, this raw, wet weather. You have eased them indeed.'

Gloomily resigned to a difficult evening meal, Father Peregrine took refuge in the kitchens, where Brother Michael was kneading a huge mound of dough. Quiet and friendly, he was a welcome alternative to the irascible Brother Andrew. He heard Peregrine's request with a smile, and found him a hunk of bread, some cheese and an apple, which Peregrine retired to a corner to eat. The kitchen staff had no leisure to watch him, and in any case were not fussy about table manners, and he ate the food gratefully and peacefully, then made his way to chapel for Vespers.

It was gloomy in the chapel, on such an evening. A few candles flickered, but in the damp air their iridescent haloes seemed to hover close to the flame, and they scarcely illuminated the dimness. Peregrine could vaguely discern figures in the abbey church, on the other side of the parish altar, but could not tell whether they would be his guests, or the usual worshippers from the village, some of whom attended Vespers as well as the morning Mass.

'*Magnificat, anima mea Dominum,*' Brother Gilbert's voice lifted in the lovely chant.

'*Et exultavit spiritus meus in Deo salutari meo,*' responded the brothers. 'My soul magnifies the Lord, and my spirit has rejoiced in God my saviour.'

'It's true,' thought Peregrine, with some surprise. 'After all the struggle of the early years, I am content now. I love this place, and these brothers committed to my charge. I am content.' He gave his mind to the chant again, which he had been singing without thinking, both words and tune being as familiar as his own skin.

'*Gloria Patri et Filio, et Spiritui Sancto . . .*'

After Vespers, as the brothers dispersed, Father Chad came round the parish altar to find the visiting family, as they sat in the gathering shadows. He led them out into the cloister, to follow Peregrine, who was crossing to his house in the persistent drizzle.

'Our lord abbot,' said Father Chad, seeing the eyes of the mother of the family watching Peregrine's awkward progress across the court.

'A crippled man?' she said in surprise. 'There must be few so afflicted who rise to become abbot of a community. He must be an extraordinary man.'

'He was not always as you see him now,' Father Chad replied, 'but he is an extraordinary man.'

They followed him into the abbot's house, and found him standing with Brother Edward before a bright fire of seasoned apple logs. The abbot's house was built with a hearth and a chimney, so that a fire might be lit to warm and cheer the guests of the abbey, though Peregrine virtually never lit it on his own account, except in the bitterest of the winter weather, when his hands, too cramped and inflexible to write well at the best of times, refused to function at all in the cold.

It was almost dark now, outside, but here the fire burned cheerily, and candles shone with a warm, soft light. The pilgrims came in gladly from the cold, and Father Chad introduced them to his superior. 'Madame de Montany and her family, Father,' he said, but Peregrine was standing staring at her, speechless, frozen to the spot.

'Clare!' he exlaimed at last.

She, too, as she saw his face, gasped with surprise and stood still.

'How came you here?' she said now. 'I had no idea . . .'

As a young boy, Peregrine du Fayel and his two older brothers had been brought up on their father Henri's manor under the wide, wild skies of the fenlands near Ely. Their neighbour, Robert de Montany, also a Norman knight, was a big kindly man, married to a gentle and sweet-tempered wife, Eloise. He had a son, Hugh, born within a week of Peregrine's birth, and a younger daughter, Louise.

On the other side of du Fayel's boundaries lay the lands of the van Moeck family, Dutch aristocracy who had settled in England on land they had inherited. They felt at home there, in the flat, wet lands under the great, luminous sky. Pieter and Gerda van Moeck had two daughters, Anne and Clare.

The children of the three households grew up together, played together as infants, rode and hunted and dined together as young people, and were all friends. Privileged young things, shielded from life's hardships, with tolerant and indulgent parents all, the world was their plaything, and they enjoyed life to the full.

When he was twenty-five years old, and she twenty-four, Geoffroi du Fayel, Peregrine's oldest brother, was betrothed to Anne van Moeck. They married and settled in a manor farm given to them by Pieter van Moeck, Anne's father, on the edge of the du Fayel lands, and from there Geoffroi took charge of the farm management of his own land, and most of his father's too. Gerda van Moeck and Melissa du Fayel, having spent the last five years discreetly engineering the match, sat back complacently to await the arrival of grandchildren, at the same time having an eye to any possible developments among their remaining offspring.

Emmanuel, the next of the du Fayel brothers, dark and quick-tempered, was by nature well adapted to bloodshed, and he took up arms in the king's service, and went away to kill as many enemies of the Crown as he could lay his hands on.

Left together, Peregrine and Hugh lived the easy lives of young noblemen, more play than work, and devoted their time to hunting and breeding horses and training falcons. Louise de Montany, a docile, home-loving body, they had little to do with, and Clare van Moeck, the youngest of them all, they tolerated and teased as a little sister, until the day of her sixteenth birthday, which was 17th March 1283.

On that day, her parents gave a banquet for her,

at which all three households gathered. Anne and Geoffroi, five years married now, were there with Pierre, their four-year-old son, and their tiny, toothless, hairless scrap of a daughter, but six weeks into the world. Emmanuel was still away, but the rest of the family was assembled.

In the solar, during the hour before they dined, Gerda van Moeck was working at her embroidery in the pale, bright sunshine that streamed through the window. Hugh and Peregrine had ridden out together, ahead of their families, partly because Hugh wanted to show off the merits of his newly acquired horse to his friend.

In age, the two young men were the same, but in every other way they were different, and Gerda van Moeck, plump and kindly, sat with her embroidery forgotten in her lap for the moment, watching them with amusement.

Hugh, big-boned, blond and gentle, with a deep voice and a hearty, generous laugh, was extolling the virtues of his new mount to Peregrine. Everything about Hugh was open, ingenuous and relaxed. Peregrine, by contrast, had a gathered, flame-like intensity about him, and the watchful, fierce expression of the falcon he was named for. Just now, his face was lit with laughter as he teased his friend, mocking him for losing his heart and his wits with it, to a mere horse.

The door of the solar opened, and Clare van Moeck shyly made her entrance, in her new dress which was her mother's birthday present to her. It was a simple gown of delphinium blue, which gave her blue eyes the depth and clarity of jewels. Her mane of rich brown hair was gathered up in a gold net, and she stood within the doorway, her lips slightly parted and her cheeks a little flushed, graceful and shy in her finery. Both young men turned their heads at the same moment and saw her, and she was utterly beautiful. From that moment, and for the rest of his life, Hugh de Montany worshipped her. But as she stood a little self-consciously before their arrested gaze, she sought Peregrine's eyes; and reading there the candid admiration she had hoped to find, her own eyes exulted. Clare van Moeck had grown into a woman, and Peregrine du Fayel wanted her.

Gerda noted with satisfaction the impact her daughter had made. Two fish on the hook; it was well. Both the banquet and the dress had proved worth the trouble.

From that day, and through the spring and summer of the year, Peregrine and Clare were more and more together. They rode and walked and talked together, having eyes only for each other. Late in the September of the year, as summer slid into autumn, there was a day when Clare stood laughing in the russet woodland and her glorious rich brown hair fell about the green gown she wore. She looked for all the world like a dryad of the autumn woods, and Peregrine took her in his arms and kissed her. Her heart triumphed. She had won him. He was hers.

With approval, their families watched their young love blossom. Another such union between the households was welcome to both the du Fayels and the van Moecks. Hugh de Montany alone could not be glad, but he kept his heartache private, continuing a steadfast friend to them both.

It was in the spring of the following year, when Clare was just seventeen, and Peregrine was twenty-four, that all this came to an end. For some little while now, the two of them had gone further in their love than they should and bedded in the fragrant bluebells in the woodland, or nestled in the warm-scented hay in the great barns of Pieter van Moeck's farm. They had lain together as lovers, wrapped in Peregrine's cloak, lost in each other and consumed in the ardour of their love.

But somehow, unexpectedly, irresistibly, came the call of God on Peregrine's soul. In the end there came a day when he held Clare in his arms and kissed her, and his face was sad but resolute as he told her his decision.

'Clare, what we have done is sin. What is between us

should have been saved for marriage. I have confessed it, for my part, to the priest, and I ask your pardon too.'

Dumbly, bewildered, she shook her head and held him close; held him fiercely as she felt in her heart that for some reason she could not understand, he was no longer hers.

'I have to leave you, my lady, my love, my heart.' He looked down at her blue eyes brimming with tears, and kissed her brow, her eyes, her cheeks, her hair; then put her away from him with a sudden, rough gesture.

'I am going to enter as a brother at St Peter's Abbey,' he said abruptly.

'A *monk*! You?' exclaimed Clare, her amazement for a moment overcoming even her sorrow. He looked at her, and she could not read the expression in his eyes, she who had thought she knew him like her own soul.

'Yes. Me,' he said simply.

He tried to explain to her later the burning of his vocation, the passionate longing which is greater than the love between man and woman, with which his soul cried out for God. She did not understand, and she wept, but she did not try to dissuade him. Neither did his disappointed and astonished parents attempt to argue with him—they had given that up when he was two years old. He was received into the community of brothers at the abbey of St Peter, near Ely, at the end of May in the year 1284, and Clare van Moeck never saw him again.

Until today.

Brother Edward was as surprised to see Clare as Peregrine was. He had known her well as a little girl, and even during his days of itinerant preaching with the Franciscans, he had been a frequent visitor to all three households. He had watched the offspring of the three families grow up through childhood and lost touch with them only when his wanderings took him as far away as the North Riding of Yorkshire, where he had finally settled.

He glanced at Peregrine, and seeing him momentarily incapable of speech, stepped forward with a welcoming smile to greet Clare.

'What a happy surprise, my dear! How the years have flown since last we met—and you are no whit less beautiful!'

'Madame de Montany,' broke in Peregrine. 'Then you married Hugh.' He had gathered his senses enough to smile at her. 'And these are Hugh's sons, yes, I see they are. The image of their father.'

'Hugh, and Edwin,' said Clare. 'And this is Melissa, my daughter—my first-born,' she added softly, with a slight tremble in her voice.

'Oh, forgive me,' said Peregrine, who had overlooked the young woman standing in the shadows at the back of the group. His words died on his lips, and his eyes widened as she stepped forward, looking at him out of intense, direct, dark grey eyes, set above a nose like a hawk's beak, a resolute mouth and a determined chin. It was like looking into a mirror.

'I am pleased to meet you, Father,' she said at last, and he held out his hand to her, like a man dreaming.

'Daughter, you are welcome,' he said, his voice barely above a whisper.

Clare held her breath as she watched Melissa take the scarred, twisted hand tenderly in both her own. What had happened to him? Melissa's hands were as his had been, scholar's hands, long and graceful; and they closed round his hand now, and released it again.

'I did not know,' he said, stating the obvious, looking from Melissa to Clare, and back again. 'I did not know. But come,' he recollected himself, 'sit down and eat. You must be hungry.'

From childhood Melissa had known the story of her father, and she well knew Henri du Fayel, Peregrine's father, whom he strongly resembled. As Melissa was so like the du Fayels, and apart from the mass of her brown hair she was so unlike either Hugh or Clare, there had seemed no point in keeping the story from her. Both Clare and Hugh had the generosity to portray her father to his little girl as a man irresistibly called by God, not as a lover who had used and abandoned his mistress. Now, the man she had wondered about all her life sat before her, and she could not take her eyes off him.

Clare, too, watched the man she had loved, and she wondered at the savage scar on his face, and her heart was wrenched with pity at his lameness, and the awkward fumbling of his hands. She watched the young brother, who waited on them at table, place the abbot's food before him, already cut up, as a mother might give cut food to a child too young to manage on his own. At the sight of that plate of food, the words of astonishment were out of her mouth before she could restrain them: 'Is that all you eat?'

She spoke with the forthright familiarity of an old friend, and one who had seen her lover many times come in from hunting, to devour a huge plate of food with the single-mindedness of an unusually fastidious wolf.

Her words broke the tension that bound the whole group, and Peregrine laughed. 'No,' he said smiling, 'but it is not easy for me to eat with guests, Clare, because of my hands.'

'What happened?' she asked, gently; and he told them, briefly, factually, and without emotion, how he came to be so maimed.

'I remember the man, and his sons,' she said, nodding her head. 'I remember the day he was taken away, and how he struggled and fought. It was awful. And this happened to you two years ago, you say?'

'Three years at Easter. I am used to it now.' These words were clearly intended to close the subject, and the talk was turned to old friends and family, and remembered places.

'Melissa is to be married this summer,' said Clare. 'She is betrothed to Ranulf Langton—do you remember the family? They are wool merchants from Thaxted. Ranulf is a fine young man.'

'You are ... twenty-five years old, this autumn it must be,' Peregrine said to Melissa. 'You have waited a while, then, to make your choice?'

'Mother always counselled me to wait for a man I felt I could really love,' replied Melissa. 'She says a marriage where one does not love would be a weary business.'

Peregrine glanced sharply at Clare, and she met his look steadily. 'Would you not think so?' she said.

'I think,' replied Peregrine carefully, 'that as the years go by, the same love would enrich *any* marriage as the love which builds and enriches a community of celibate monks; and that is the love which is pledged to lay down its own wants and preferences for the sake of the other. The marriage that was built on natural affection, and had nothing of such love would, in the end, sour, however promising its beginning, I think.'

Clare's son laughed. 'But you are not recommending, sir, that one should marry regardless of inclination or affection, unless one has to? That would seem noble, but not entirely sensible.'

Peregrine smiled at him: 'Edwin, heaven help me, I am a monk. It is not for me to advance opinions on marriage! All I am saying is that between any people, if their love has not that Christ-like quality of humble service, then neither is it built to last for ever.'

'Of course,' said Clare, 'even where your heart is given to love and to serve, it does not always follow that the one you love will be true to you, or to his own protestations of love. Men change, and love given does not guarantee love returned.'

Peregrine dropped his gaze before her, his face ashamed.

'No,' he said, 'I know.' He was silent.

'So you are travelling to Iona,' remarked Edward cheerfully. 'A beautiful place. Would that I could celebrate the Easter feast there with you. But you have chosen rough weather for your journey.'

Young Hugh laughed; a laugh so like his father's that

Peregrine looked up, startled; it was as though his old friend sat there with them in the person of his son.

'Brother, we do not choose our weather,' said the young man. 'Pray for us, and the one who sends the rain may relent a little!'

They talked a while longer, over the remains of their meal, and then it was time for the brothers to go to Compline, the day's last office, after which the monastery was folded into the Great Silence, and no conversation at all was permitted until the following day.

The pilgrims meant to rise early in the morning and be ready to depart as soon as they had heard Mass, so Edwin, Hugh and Melissa returned to the guest house, taking the chance to retire early and rest in preparation for their journey. Clare said she would come to Compline first, and then join them. Father Chad and Brother Edward went with the young people to the guest house to see that all they needed had been prepared for them. Peregrine set off directly to the church taking a little longer than the others to make his way there; and Clare walked with him, suiting her pace to his slow and laborious progress.

'Why did you never tell me?' he said.

'Because you would have married me,' she responded sadly, 'and I couldn't bear to live my life as your second best, your dutiful choice. I kept it a secret until it could be kept a secret no longer, and by then you were clothed, and had taken your vows as a novice, and it was too late. I made them promise not to tell you.'

'So you married Hugh.'

'He offered immediately, to save me from shame.'

'And two fine sons he has given you. You have found him a good husband, I think.'

'Oh yes, he has been to me all that a husband should be,' she said softly, 'but you—'

'Clare, don't say it!' he cried, harshly.

'I have Melissa always to remind me. Every turn of her head and gesture of her hands is yours. That spring ... how could I forget?'

He flashed her one glance and then looked away. 'Neither have I forgotten,' he said quietly, 'and it does me no good, and does nothing for my peace of mind, to remember.'

They parted outside the great black bulk of the abbey church, he to take his place among the community, and she to go into the church, where visitors and parishioners sat, divided by the wooden screen and the parish altar from the brethren. She watched him go, lame and jerky on his crutch. He did not look back.

The de Montanys were ready to depart the next morning. They attended Mass in the abbey church, and made ready their horses with saddle and pack while the brothers were in chapter. By the time chapter was over, Hugh and Edwin and Clare's maid were mounted, and their groom stood holding the bridles of Clare's and Melissa's horses as well as his own. Edward came across the court to them, to bid them farewell, and Clare, after a little hesitation, went to find Peregrine in his lodging, hurt that he had not come to say goodbye.

'The time has come. We must leave,' she said. He stood and looked at her without speaking.

'Will you give me the kiss of peace?'

Slowly, he shook his head. 'I wish you peace, Clare, with all my heart; but embrace you I will not.'

'Then shake my hand, at least,' she said, her voice trembling.

'No, Clare! Do not ask me to touch you. There is too much between us still, you know it as well as I do! Go in peace, but for pity's sake, go!'

She looked at him once more, and then turned swiftly and left, without another word.

Outside, growing impatient in the steady drizzling rain, Hugh and Edwin sent Melissa after their mother to hurry her along. Melissa came to the door as her mother came out.

'A moment, and I will be with you, Mother,' she said. 'I must just say goodbye.'

Clare nodded, and went to join her family, and

Melissa, hesitantly entering the abbot's house, found him standing still in the middle of the room, his hand pressed to his mouth, and his eyes bright with tears. Struggling for composure, he stretched out his hand to her, and tried to smile.

'I'm glad, so glad we came,' she said. 'I think we have made things difficult for you, but everything is different for me, now. Before, my father was a stranger, but now I belong. And I'm sorry it hurts you so, but I'm glad you still love Mother.'

She had taken his hand in both of hers, and she looked into his face with tenderness and happiness.

'Go in peace,' he whispered. 'God bless you, little one.'

She looked at him steadily one more moment, then, 'Goodbye,' she said, and was gone.

The rest of the party was waiting for her impatiently. She hastily embraced Edward, saying gaily, 'Goodbye, Uncle Edward! I shall be back!' and added in a whisper, 'Go and help him when we're gone. He needs someone.'

Brother Edward watched them ride out, cloaked and hooded against the dismal mist of rain, then turned back to the abbot's lodging where he found Peregrine preparing parchment and inks for Brother Theodore, who was coming to do some writing at his dictation, later in the morning. Peregrine looked at Edward with a carefully composed expression of polite enquiry.

'Yes, Brother?'

'Father, there is no need to pretend,' said Edward bluntly. 'It would have devastated me, too.'

'Pray for me,' said Peregrine, and that was all he said.

They expected to hear no more of the de Montany family, at least for some while, but barely three weeks later, just before Easter, in the chill, grey evening of a cold March day, Brother Edward overtook Peregrine on his way to Vespers, breathless with hurry and agitation.

'Father, Melissa de Montany is here! She has ridden far and is in great distress. She is asking for you.'

Peregrine turned back immediately for the gatehouse,

where he found Melissa, her hands twisting in her lap, her face white and her eyes shadowed with suffering and lack of sleep. He came and sat beside her, his eyes searching hers with concern.

'What is this?' he said. 'What has happened?'

'She is dead!' Melissa blurted out. 'Mother is dead! We came to a village not three days' ride from here, and stayed at the inn there. Their food was dreadful, greasy and foul. The meat stank. We were all taken ill; it was poisoning from the meat, I think. Hugh and Edwin were tossing and delirious with fever for days. They are recovered now, but too weak yet to ride. I had eaten scarcely anything and was not too bad; but Mother died! She is dead!'

Peregrine gathered her wordlessly in his arms, and she clung to him. 'She is dead! She is dead!' she moaned over and over, and shook violently as he held her. Finally, she ceased to speak, and pressing her face to his breast, she sobbed and sobbed. Cradling her, he laid his cheek on her hair, and closed his eyes silently on his own tears.

He held her and comforted her through many such storms in the week that followed, as she grieved and wept for her mother. She leaned on his understanding love as on a rock, and when Hugh and Edwin came to fetch her, and began the sad journey homewards to bear the news to their father, the pilgrimage forgotten, she was sufficiently in command of herself to travel with them. Through the nights, Peregrine had kept vigil in the chapel and prayed for her, and during the days he had stayed with her, quietly watching over her, asking nothing, but allowing her to grieve.

She embraced him gratefully as they parted.

'Thank you, Father,' she said. 'Thank you so much. May we meet in happier times!'

He nodded. 'Greet Hugh for me. Tell him ... tell him I'm sorry.'

Edward and Peregrine stood together to watch the

forlorn little party ride away at first light on a grey, chill day, then walked slowly to the chapel for Mass.

Edward looked at Peregrine's face, haggard with exhaustion and grief. 'You have strengthened and comforted her,' said Edward. When Peregrine did not reply, Edward looked at the sad, tired face, and added gently, 'And you? Whom will you allow to comfort you in your own grief?'

Peregrine stopped and looked at him wearily. 'Surely Christ has borne our griefs, and carried all our sorrows,' he said quietly, and then groaned, 'but oh, my God, my God, it takes some believing.'

Mother was quiet.

'Is that all?' I exploded. 'Didn't Melissa ever come back? What happened next? Oh Mother, there must be more!'

'She came back. She married Ranulf Langton, and had children of her own, and some years later, just before the birth of her youngest child, she came to make her home in Yorkshire, and she visited them often. I told you, you remember, that Brother Edward told these stories first to his great-niece, who was your long ago great-grandmother Melissa.'

'Oh, but Mother, it's so sad! Tell me some more, don't leave it there!'

'Sad? Yes I suppose so. All the stories are sad, in a way. I don't believe there's a one of them without tears and struggle; but that was the life, you see. It wasn't easy. Saying sorry, and giving up your own way, and daily turning your back on your own wants took some doing. But now, help your Daddy with the drying up and I'll tell you a quick story to cheer you up again.'

As I got to my feet to take Mother's coffee cup out to the kitchen, there was a thunder of footsteps on the path outside, the front door burst open, and Mary and Beth piled in through the doorway, breathless with running, their cheeks pink and their eyes shining.

'We're home!' shouted Beth.

'Therese buyed us an ice-cream!' cried Mary excitedly, 'and it had a stalk!'

Therese was some minutes behind them. 'They can run like the wind, those two!' she exclaimed. 'Is the kettle on, Melissa? I'm dying for a cup of tea.'

'Any minute now,' I replied, and went on my way into the kitchen.

'Oh, Daddy, you've done it all! I was supposed to be helping you.'

He was sitting in the armchair in the corner, reading his paper, with the dog lying on his feet, and the cat curled up on his lap. He looked at me over the top of his glasses.

'I am among you as one who serves,' he said, in an exaggerated tone of suffering self-righteousness. 'You can make me a cup of tea, though. Once your Mother gets going, time's forgotten. I never knew such a woman, she could talk the hind leg off a donkey.'

'A donkey?' said Mary, a little uncertainly. She had come into the kitchen and was leaning affectionately on Daddy's arm. 'Why?'

'Just a figure of speech, my poppet,' said Daddy smiling at her. 'Get cracking with that tea, Melissa, you look as though you're in a trance!'

As the kettle boiled, there came an angry bellow from upstairs, 'I . . . WANT . . . MUMMY!' Cecily was awake. She came stumping down the stairs, only just awake, her limbs still unco-ordinated, and her face still flushed from sleep.

'I . . . WANT . . . MUMMY!' she roared again, but when Mother came out of the living-room, laughing at her, she was so incensed at not being taken seriously that she flung herself on the floor in the passage way, her legs rigid and her little hands clenched into fists, making a noise like rending metal.

Mother sighed. 'Heigh-ho. Back to reality,' she said resignedly. 'Oh, come on, Cecily! Do get up.'

Just then, there was a knock at the front door. Cecily leapt to her feet, crying, 'IwanttoopenitIwanttoopenit

Iwanttoopenit!' but the front door was opened before she got there, by our Grandma, who was on the other side of it.

Cecily burst into wails of disappointment and frustration, tears pouring down her crimson face, the veins standing out on her neck like cords. Grandma, confronted with this sight, looked down in astonishment for a moment, then knelt down on the floor and held out her arms. 'Cecily, my darling!' she said. 'What's the matter, poppet? Have you hurt yourself?'

Cecily was too much beside herself to speak.

'I think she wanted to open the front door, Grandma,' Therese explained.

'Oh, I see. Right-o, then.' Grandma hastily went out again, closed the door firmly behind her, and knocked on it loudly, calling through the letter-box, 'Is anyone at home?'

There was a moment's pause while Cecily wondered whether to relent. Grandma knocked again. With a hoarse cry of joy, Cecily ran and opened the front door, the noise and tears magically evaporated, her little face dimpling in an enchanting smile, her great blue eyes shining.

'Oh, hello, Cecily!' cried Grandma. 'Can I come in for a cup of tea, darling, please?'

'Grandma,' cooed Cecily. Mother shook her head and sighed.

'Make the big pot of tea, Melissa,' she said, 'and there's a new packet of chocolate digestives in the cupboard. It's hidden at the back, behind the macaroni.'

The rest of the afternoon was whiled away comfortably, chatting to Grandma and playing snakes and ladders with Mary and Beth. Grandma tried to teach Cecily how to play snap, but Cecily didn't want to put any of her cards down. She wouldn't say 'Snap' when the cards were the same, but she got cross if Grandma said 'Snap' and tried to pick them up.

That was typical of Cecily. We sighed, looked at each other and laughed.

V

THE MOULTING FALCON

Therese's friend Lilian Shepherd came during the afternoon, to ask if Therese wouldn't mind helping her with her English homework. Lilian was a very popular girl at school, and always had a group of friends around her, so Therese was rather flattered that Lilian especially sought her friendship, even though there was something indefinable she didn't quite like about Lilian. Mary and Beth thought she was wonderful, because she was tall and slim and stunningly attractive, with great big eyes like a startled faun's, and a rippling mane of silky blonde hair. Mother and Daddy both disliked Lilian intensely, and Mother said all she was looking for from Therese was a brain transplant. I myself couldn't help admiring her, although she wasn't very nice to the little girls; but that might have been because Cecily had bitten her once, for no reason that anyone could tell.

Therese took her into the kitchen and made her some coffee, and as Lilian sipped it, she explained that she hadn't quite been able to come up with any ideas for her essay on Hopkins' poetry and wondered if Therese had any thoughts. ... She had read a little, she said, and really hadn't got anywhere with it. Perhaps she would be able to borrow Therese's essay, just to have a look at it? She thought it might help to inspire her.

Therese, who loved Hopkins, was delighted to lend

Lilian her essay, and asked if Lilian would let her know what her own thoughts about the poems were, when she'd got a bit further. Lilian smiled and said she was sure her thoughts would not be half as original as Therese's, and then she excused herself and slipped off home with Therese's essay. I was bursting with indignation.

'Therese, you are a goose! She's going to copy it!' I exclaimed. 'Why did you let her have it?'

Therese looked at me uncertainly. 'You don't think she will, do you? She only said she wanted to read it. She couldn't copy it, Mrs Freeman would know.'

Mother came in with all the dirty tea things, and asked what Lilian had come for.

'What was it this time? Your Hopkins essay?'

'Mother! How did you know?'

'Because I'm not as daft as you. She's in your English class, isn't she? Be a bit more sensible, Therese. She'll get you into trouble one of these days. Don't have too much to do with her.'

'Whenever Lilian's been here,' I said, 'she always leaves an uncomfortable feeling behind. It's funny, because she doesn't argue or anything.'

'But she's my friend!' said Therese, a bit upset.

Mother began to run washing-up water into the bowl. 'Be friendly, Therese; there's nothing wrong with that, but be a bit wary, that's all. Now then, Daddy is going to run Grandma home in a minute, and take me to Evensong. Cecily can come with Daddy for the ride, but will you see to Mary's and Beth's baths for me? Daddy will do their bedtime when he gets in.'

Therese said she would, and I asked if I could come to Evensong with Mother.

'Of course you can come! Get your shoes on, though, and brush your hair, because we must go in five minutes.'

I loved Evensong. I loved the stillness of the church that enfolded the small evening congregation. The mellow evening sunshine that slanted in low through the windows in summer, the gathering, sombre shadows of spring and autumn evenings, and the profounder darkness of the winter months, all wrapped the evening worship in a mystery and a beauty that I never found in the brightness and bustle of family service in the morning.

Our church was just on the edge of the town, set in a pretty little remnant of woodland, a tiny drift of countryside still left in peace by the urban sprawl. Daddy dropped us off at the end of the church path, and we stood to wave goodbye to Cecily as he drove away. It was very important to Cecily to say 'goodbye'. If she thought she had not made her farewells properly, she would scream deafeningly until Daddy turned the car back. So we waved until they turned the corner, and then strolled up the path to the church and into the stone porch.

The great wooden inner door opened with a click as Mother pushed it. Charlie Page, the blacksmith, was always the sidesman in the evening, and his face, freckled with age, wrinkled in a smile as he gave us our hymnbooks and prayer-books. Mother settled into our pew with a happy sigh. The evening service was a cherished time for her, when she could give herself to the worship without the stress of the little ones' company, or the anxiety of being late. Whenever we went anywhere as a family, however much time we gave ourselves to get ready, we were always late, and Mother hated it.

In the pew behind ours sat Mrs Crabtree; a tall, well-built, energetic, silver-haired lady in her middle seventies. She had borne six children in her time, and was still motherly through and through, wise and kind, with a rich, ready laugh. Unfortunately her singing was more out of tune than any I have ever heard before or since, and I set my teeth to endure as the organist struck up for the first hymn:

> Glory to thee, my God, this night,
> For all the blessings of the light.
> Keep me, O keep me, King of kings,
> Beneath thine own almighty wings.

I knew about his almighty wings. They were folding around us here, in the quiet of the evening, kind and everlasting and utterly secure. It was the same wings that wrapped me round in our home, in the bedtime candle-light. Sanctuary from the busy and complicated daytime, God gathered us under his evening wing, haven for all our weariness.

The evening service felt as familiar as an old friend, comfortable to be with. I knew the prayers and the responses without looking at the book. Actually, I could say them all while thinking about something completely different, which to my shame I frequently did.

'My soul doth magnify the Lord: and my spirit hath rejoiced in God my Saviour,' we sang.

I thought of Peregrine, singing the same words, but in Latin, all those years ago; wrapped like me in the contentment of evening calm, blissfully unaware of the turbulence of surprise and grief that lay around the corner ... 'No!' I told myself sharply, 'this is not the time! Come out of the walled garden, and shut the door firmly behind you, and turn your back on it. Concentrate.'

'Glory be to the Father, and to the Son ...' Mrs Crabtree sang vigorously behind me.

Father Carnforth took the evening service. His gentle, wheezy old voice led us through the prayers; the Lord's prayer, the responses, the collect of the day. I felt reassured by the humble confidence with which he prayed.

'Give unto thy servants that peace which the world cannot give ...'

What a gift! What a thing to ask for! And yet, incredibly, it is given. I knew that peace; I had been brought up with the flavour and the texture of it in our home. Peace, at the very core of things, constant, unobtrusive, like the humming of the fridge and the ticking of the clock. Peace, freely given. Beyond our making, or even our understanding. *Thank you, God.*

Father Carnforth was climbing slowly into the pulpit for his sermon. He read his sermons out of a book, very fast. He was in unspoken agreement with his congregation that the preaching of sermons was an unavoidable bore; to be endured uncomplainingly, but not prolonged. Tonight's offering was about the textual background of the Synoptic Gospels, and I strongly suspected from the way he read it that it was as incomprehensible to him as it was to us. He shut the book with a snap and laid it aside with obvious relief, as he announced the final hymn: 'The day thou gavest, Lord, is ended. The darkness falls at thy behest. Hymn number 277.'

Mrs Crabtree gave joyful tongue behind me. Did God mind that dreadful singing, he who made the nightingale and the lark? Probably not. Probably it was the soul of Mrs Crabtree he was listening to, the worshipping song of her heart, and that rang true as a bell.

Then it was over, and we went out into the cool of the evening. Father Carnforth smiled kindly at me, and shook my hand in his aged hand, the joints swollen with arthritis and the skin wrinkled and discoloured with the years. His nose was big and red, with dark whiskers growing from it, and he was almost completely bald. He smelt strongly of pipe tobacco, and his cassock was not quite clean, but even Cecily loved him, who had strong opinions about most people. His friendship with Cecily was helped along by the bag of peppermints he carried in his pocket, but it was not entirely that. He called her his sugar-plum fairy. Mary, who was always very worried about people she loved growing old and dying, focused her anxiety on him, as the most ancient person of her acquaintance.

Father Carnforth looked at me with his watery old eyes. They were brown, and small, and twinkling. Hedgehog's eyes. Like Mother's, they looked into the middle of you and could make you feel uncomfortable at times.

'Ah, Melissa, you do me good, you're a breath of springtime,' he wheezed at me. 'Tell your little Mary that Father Carnforth is still clinging to this world and sends his love.'

He shook Mother's hand: 'Goodnight, my dear. Take care.'

Mother and I walked slowly down the pathway, breathing in the scent of the roses that grew in a hedge around the churchyard.

'I often think how odd it is,' she mused, 'that Lilian Shepherd is tall and graceful, with hair like spun gold and a face like a Greek goddess, while Father Carnforth is old and bald and fat and wrinkled; but it is Father Carnforth who is beautiful, not Lilian.'

'It's you that's odd, Mother!' I replied as I took her arm, 'and beautiful. Will you tell me that story on the way home? The one you were going to tell me.'

'Melissa, your appetite for stories is almost as prodigious as Cecily's appetite for sweets! I will tell you the story on one condition, and that is that you pester me for no more stories today.'

I promised happily. Mother picked a white deadnettle from the side of the path and pulled off one of its creamy flowers. 'Did you know,' she said, 'that if you suck at the base of the flower, you get a drop of nectar from it—that's unless the bees have been before you, of course. Try it and see.' She showed me how to suck out the nectar, and gave me the nettle stem. I tried one of the flowers, and was astonished by the sweet, light, delicious flavour of the nectar.

'Now you know what bees eat,' said Mother, and while I worked my way through the rest of the flowers on the stem, we walked slowly out of the churchyard, and started homewards up the hill.

'It was a time when Father Peregrine was tired, and very sad,' began Mother. 'Just a minute. I've got a stone in my shoe.' She held on to my shoulder while she took it off and shook out the stone, then we walked on again.

It was only three days after Melissa had gone back home with Hugh and Edwin, and Father Peregrine had been plunged into a valley of despair: grief, temptation and sorrow. Every night during the week she had stayed with them he had kept watch and prayed for her before the altar in the chapel; and during the days he had put aside everything but the daily round of prayer to look after her, snatching an hour's sleep here and there, fasting the greater part of each day.

On the day she left, a cloth merchant and his wife who were travelling past came seeking hospitality at the abbey. Peregrine had to entertain them at lunch and supper, disciplining himself to chat about trivial matters and show an interest in the ups and downs of the cloth trade. Also, the rent re-assessment and lease renewal for the farm tenancies belonging to the abbey must be made by Lady Day, so Peregrine had spent two arduous days in conference about the rents with Brother Ambrose, the cellarer, who looked after the finances of the abbey as well as the distribution of clothing, bed linen and other necessities. They had also discussed the provision of hospitality for the pilgrims and visitors who would be guests of the abbey during the Easter Feast.

After all this, he felt weary and numb, drained now of emotion. The old wounds in his leg were aching badly, since to keep himself awake as he prayed through the long nights he had forced the unyielding knee to kneel. So his back also was tense and aching, and he had a persistent, nagging headache just to round everything off. In the end, Brother Edward insisted that he come to the infirmary and submit to having his back and leg rubbed with oils of lavender, bergamot and geranium.

'Don't be ridiculous,' snapped Peregrine. 'I'm a monk, not a lady of the court. Save your aromatics for the sick, Edward.'

'I won't have to save them long if you carry on like this,' insisted Brother Edward stoutly. 'It's you who will be ill if you don't heed my advice. This week long you've not had those hands of yours attended to. Prayer and fasting are all very well, but you're not adding common sense to the recipe. You can't possibly undertake your responsibility to this community when you're half dead with fatigue and aching from head to foot!'

'How do you know I ache?' mumbled Peregrine grudgingly.

'Because I have eyes in my head and wits to understand what I see. Now, Father, you hear sense, and come to me in the infirmary.'

Peregrine sighed and would say no more, so Brother Edward left him, muttering crossly about his stubbornness. By the afternoon, however, Father Peregrine felt ill enough to give in. He made his way slowly down the cobbled path that bordered the kitchen gardens. A few gilly-flowers grew there, perfuming the air with their intoxicating scent, and among the cobbles, little hearts-ease plants grew, and a few violets still. He leaned heavily on his crutch, and his lame leg felt like a lead weight. In the kitchen garden, the young vegetable plants were in, and Brother Tom was hoeing the immaculate beds. He watched Father Peregrine toiling down the path, looking as though he could hardly drag himself along.

Peregrine said afterwards that it was his own fault, that he should have been paying attention to what he was doing. A loose cobble turned under the crutch as he leaned on it, and it shot awkwardly to the side, tripping him so that he fell on his face on the ground.

Brother Tom saw him fall, dropped his hoe and ran to help. With his support, Peregrine got slowly to his feet, and Tom restored his crutch to him so he could stand. His nose was bleeding and the left side of his face grazed badly. He said nothing, but stood there, dazed. He blinked, and sighed. He took Tom's proffered handkerchief (which was none too clean) with stiff difficulty into his hand, and clamped it to his bleeding nose.

'Come, Father,' said Tom, 'I'll help you. Come into the infirmary and sit down.' He took Peregrine's free arm, and half led him, half supported him, to the infirmary. The door stood open and, just within, a doorway to the right led off the passage way into a room where a bench was placed near the door. Peregrine slumped onto it without speaking, his lame leg stretched in front of him, looking blackly out at the world over the grubby handkerchief Tom had given him.

It occurred to Tom as he looked at him that he looked remarkably like a moulting falcon; dishevelled and out of sorts, and with that same fierce, brooding look in his eye. Half sorry for him and half amused in spite of himself, Tom hovered beside him a moment, wondering whether to go in search of Brother Edward.

As he stood hesitating, one of the lay servants, Martin Jonson, a cheerful, good-hearted young man from the village, bustled into the room from the doorway on the other side. His arms were so full of clean linen for the infirmary beds that he could scarcely see over the top of the pile, on which rested his chin. He saw Peregrine, however, and came to a halt in front of him.

'Dear, dear, dear; what have we here, Father?' he asked jovially, using the same jolly and encouraging tone with which he was used to addressing the senile and ailing inhabitants of the infirmary. 'Whatever have you been and gone and done to yourself?'

Father Peregrine regarded him coldly over the top of the gory handkerchief. 'I fell od the stodes add gave byself a dose-bleed,' he said with icy dignity.

'Don't worry Father, we'll put you back together in no time!' responded Martin cheerfully, and moved purposefully towards the doorway. 'I'll go and find Brother Edward for you, Father,' he said, but he never made it to the door. Peregrine's face was visible to him, but not his feet, and not noticing the stiff, lame leg that stuck out across his pathway, he tripped over it and fell among an avalanche of bedding.

Peregrine gave an involuntary yell of pain as the man's weight hit his leg, and then his teeth gritted and his eyes screwed shut. He swore. Brother Tom's eyes widened at the string of inventive oaths that streamed from his abbot's lips. He was astonished (and delighted) to hear the words he himself used in moments of weakness in the mouth of his superior, normally so courteously and quietly spoken.

Great-uncle Edward, who had come hurrying to see what all the fuss was about, was not so delighted, and clicked his tongue disapprovingly. 'For shame, Father,' he said. 'Martin, get off his leg, man and pick this lot up. Brother Thomas, you might assist him rather than stand there gawping. Really, some of you lads are about as much use as two left feet! On second thoughts, fetch me a basin of water, when you can get through the doorway.'

Tom helped Martin pick up his pile of washing, and went for the bowl of water.

'I ask your pardon, Father,' Martin said apologetically. 'I trust you are not too badly hurt?'

Peregrine looked at him with a sickly attempt at a smile, and shook his head.

'For myself, I must say I was winded, but this here bed-linen broke my fall,' continued Martin, slightly peeved that nobody seemed particularly concerned with his own well-being.

'Thank you, Martin; just take the linen and put it away, there's a good lad,' said Edward patiently, and Martin departed, narrowly avoiding a collision with Tom in the corridor, as he returned bearing the basin of water.

'Let me look at your leg first, Father,' said Edward. 'That was a hefty weight to go crashing down on it. How is it?'

'It *hurts*,' Peregrine almost shouted at him, then sighed, 'Oh, I'b sorry Edward, but what a foolish questiod.'

'Brother Thomas, take a cloth from the cupboard there and clean his face while I have a look at this leg. Yes, that is a magnificent bruise, my friend. It will be all the colours of the sunset in a day or two, but no real harm done. You'll do.'

Tom removed the blood-soaked handkerchief, and gently washed Peregrine's face in the cool water. 'Keep your head back, Father. Your nose still bleeds slightly. Yes, that goes better.'

'What are you gridding at?' asked Peregrine sourly, looking out of ferocious dark eyes at Tom's face bent over him.

'You!' said Tom, laughing, as he carefully washed the grit from the graze on Peregrine's face. 'You've just the same disagreeable look about you as a moulting falcon— "touch me not for I'd peck you!"'

'Brother Thomas!' exclaimed Edward. 'How can you speak with such disrespect? Recollect whom you're addressing and be a little less familiar in your speech, please! How did you come to do this, Father?'

'I fell od—hag od a bidit, let be blow by dose.' He fished in his pocket for his own handkerchief, and cautiously blew his nose. 'That's better. A loose cobble on the path by the vegetable gardens turned under my crutch, and I fell. Thank you, Brother Thomas, I feel more like a human being again. Moulting falcon indeed—I'll wager you don't speak with such impudence to Father Matthew ... I was on my way, Brother Edward, to beg pardon for my rude refusal of your kindness, and ask if you will after all give my back and leg a rub with your oils. I feel like a wrecked ship.'

They patched him up, put ointment on the graze on his face, and arnica on the wonderful bruises with which he and Martin between them had decorated his legs, and Edward massaged his hands and back and leg for him with his aromatic oils. Under the capable manipulation of Edward's strong and practised hands, Peregrine relaxed, and as the tension flowed out of him, he fell asleep. They left him to sleep all afternoon and evening.

He was back in his stall in chapel for Compline and the night Office, and by the time Divine Office was concluded and it was time for community chapter, he was more himself again—albeit rather battered-looking—presiding over the meeting of the community with his accustomed attentiveness and authority.

The chapter began as usual, with the confession by the novices of any faults they may have committed. At Father Matthew's prompting, Brother Thaddeus came, embarrassed and self-conscious, to kneel before the community.

'Brothers, I humbly confess my fault,' he said. 'I ... stubbed my toe yesterday ...' he paused.

'Hell's teeth!' muttered Brother Cormac to Brother Francis. 'Is it an offence even to stub your toe now?'

'... and I said ... I said ... I used a most vile oath,' continued Thaddeus. 'I ask God's forgiveness and yours, brothers, for the offence.'

It fell to the abbot, on these occasions, to pronounce God's forgiveness, and Father Peregrine sat for a long moment, regarding Thaddeus as he knelt before them. Thaddeus began to sweat. Then Peregrine looked across at Father Matthew with a curious expression on his face. He sighed, picked up the crutch that lay on the floor beside him, and got slowly to his feet. He crossed over, before the puzzled eyes of the community (puzzled, that is, except for Brother Tom, who was grinning like an idiot, and Brother Edward), to where Brother Thaddeus knelt, looking up at his abbot apprehensively.

'Stubbed your toe?' he said, looking down at him. 'I trust you are quite recovered.'

'Yes thank you, Father,' mumbled Thaddeus, wondering what on earth this was about. Leaning heavily on his shoulder, Peregrine bent with a grimace of pain to kneel beside him.

'I humbly confess my fault,' he said. 'Brothers, I also was guilty of using some of the most depraved language yesterday; in the hearing, furthermore, of one of our lay servants and one of our novices. I ask your forgiveness, and God's.'

There followed a startled silence, which Father Peregrine broke by saying testily, 'I believe in the circumstances, Father Chad, it falls to you to pronounce God's forgiveness.'

'Oh! Oh, yes. I—I'm sorry!' stuttered Father Chad. 'God forgives you, my brothers, and so do we.'

Father Peregrine, leaning again on Thaddeus, rose painfully to his feet, and limped back to his place.

The novices withdrew, as was customary, leaving the fully professed brothers to continue the community chapter.

'He didn't have to do that,' said Brother Francis. 'He could have waited until we'd gone.'

'It was more honest, though,' said Thaddeus, 'and it was worth it just to see Father Matthew's face! What *did* he say, anyway, Tom?'

Tom shook his head and wagged a finger at them in mock reproval. 'One man's sin,' he said, 'is not an appropriate topic for another man's conversation: and besides, it would make me blush to repeat it!'

We turned the corner into our road, and the evening sun had transformed the window-panes of all the houses into sheets of gold.

'That was the last time Father Matthew ever insisted that one of the novices confess to the whole community for swearing,' finished Mother, with a smile. 'Run on ahead, Melissa, love, and put the kettle on.'

VI
THE ASCENDING LARK

Mary's birthday was on September the twenty-ninth, the feast of St Michael and all Angels. Last year her birthday had fallen on a Sunday, but that year, the year she was six, her birthday fell on a school day. It was a warm, clear morning, and Mary sat like a princess at the breakfast table, wearing her best dress and her happiest smile as she looked at her little pile of presents that lay among their tissue wrappings on the table in front of her.

Mary's smile (even now she is a grown woman it is still the same) has always been a smile of extraordinary loveliness, transforming her thin, serious face into something quite dazzling.

There was not the money for large or expensive presents, but Therese and I had sewn her a doll with a pretty dress and bonnet. The fiddly bits were slightly grubby from the sweat of our concentration, and I had left a bloodstain from a pricked finger on the doll's face, but Mary didn't seem to notice. She loved it, and she loved the necklace that Mother had saved from her own childhood, and the blue cardigan Grandma had knitted to match Mary's best dress. She loved everything. I can remember thinking, with a twinge of guilt at my cynicism, how easily pleased you are when you're only six.

Mary sighed a huge sigh of contentment, and then turned her attention to the menu for tea. We were allowed to choose whatever we liked, within reason, for our birthday teas, and usually spent weeks beforehand deciding and planning and changing our minds—yes, even Therese and I, although we pretended to be so grown-up as to be above such things.

Mary was quite sure what she wanted. She raised her small, determined chin and fixed her earnest grey eyes on Mother's face. 'I would like orang-outang pie,' she said, very firmly.

Mother looked slightly at a loss.

'What did you say, Mary?' asked Therese.

'Orang-outang pie,' repeated Mary, her voice faltering a little as she read the bewilderment on our faces. 'I would like orang-outang pie.'

Mother's face cleared and she began to laugh, 'Oh, Mary! You mean lemon meringue pie!'

The wave of our laughter shattered Mary's fragile dignity, and she began to cry.

'Mary, my love, of course you shall have it,' said Mother, trying to compose her face. 'Is there anything else you would like especially?'

'Candles,' whispered Mary, abashed, 'on my cake.'

'There will be candles!' promised Mother. 'And lemon meringue pie. Now make haste to school, girls, or you'll be late.'

Therese and I took Mary and Beth down as far as the county primary school, and stayed to wave goodbye to them as they went in at the gate. Mary was happy again when we left her, still wearing her best dress and a crown of marigolds. Her eyes shone like candles, and her head was held high as she walked down the path to the school building, clutching her bag which held her birthday treasures, ready to show the teacher. We watched them go, and then continued on our way to the high school for girls.

The school motto which decorated our blazer pockets was the same as that of the Royal Air Force, *Per ardua ad astra*, exhorting us through hard work to reach for the stars. It was a school proud of its academic record, and all the lovely possibilities of that motto were ignored in favour of the one dry interpretation, 'Pass your exams.' The only stars we were encouraged to yearn for within those walls were the little gold, gummed-paper shapes that the younger pupils earned for good work.

Since it was Monday, I was condemned to failure by the time-table before I even entered the gates: geography, chemistry, French, and a double lesson of mathematics. The day was redeemed marginally by an English lesson at the end of the afternoon. I struggled through a confusion of isobars, alkaline reaction, *petits dialogues*, and trigonometry, to collapse wearily into my chair for the English lesson, with a sigh of relief. We were spending the autumn term studying the English Romantic poets, and the present focus of our attention was Shelley. We had been reading his poetry for two weeks now—or rather listening to Mrs Freeman read it. We took up where we had left off the previous lesson, halfway through the romantic wallowings of the tragic tale 'Rosalind and Helen'.

Mrs Freeman ploughed on and on through stanza after stanza, and the self-indulgent, purple language at first annoyed me, then began to seem unbearable, and finally hilarious. Mrs Freeman's voice shook with emotion as she flicked over to page 188, the class meekly following her progress in their dog-eared, ink-stained textbooks, yellowed with age.

> 'And first, I felt my fingers sweep
> The harp, and a long quivering cry
> Burst from my lips in symphony ...'

Mrs Freeman declaimed in low and trembling tones.

> '... The dusk and solid air was shaken
> As swift and swifter the notes came
> From my touch that wandered like quick flame,
> And from my bosom labouring
> With some unutterable thing.

> The awful sound of my own voice made
> My lips tremble—

'Is something the matter, Melissa?' Mrs Freeman stopped in mid-flow and fixed me with a look of withering contempt. I could no more control the broad grin on my face than I had been able to restrain the snort of laughter that had escaped from me.

'Melissa? Something is amusing you? Perhaps you would explain to the class?'

'I'm sorry, Mrs Freeman,' I gasped, trying to conquer the waves of mirth that were still rising. 'It's nothing really. It's just ... it's just ... well, the poetry's so silly!'

Mrs Freeman looked at me in silence, and I felt the tension as she weighed up in her mind whether to approach the situation with an Enlightened Class Discussion, or to treat it as a Very Serious Matter. I was lucky. She plumped for the former.

'What a very interesting comment, Melissa. Can you explain just what you mean? Shelley's poetry has been loved and revered by the learned and the great, and yet you find it "silly"?'

'It *is* silly,' I said, with a sudden flash of reckless irritation. 'He takes himself too seriously. It's as though he's forgotten how to laugh at himself, so that it's not real any more, like when Beth, my little sister, is in a bad mood and goes off into Mother's bedroom to practise making miserable faces in the mirror. And not only that; my mother says—'

I stopped. There was a dangerous glint in Mrs Freeman's eye. Maybe she wouldn't want to hear what Mother had to say on the subject of Shelley's poetry.

'Yes?' said Mrs Freeman, but her tone of voice was not all that encouraging, 'And what does your mother say, Melissa?'

'Mother says, that love is only true love when it shows itself in fidelity—um, faithfulness. She says if a person has the feeling of love, but no faithfulness, his love is just self-indulgent sentimentality. And that's what Shelley was like, isn't it? He wrote fine poems to his wife and his lovers, but he wasn't a faithful man. So how can his poetry about love be worth anything if his love in real life wasn't worth anything?'

'Well, I understand what you're trying to say, Melissa,' said Mrs Freeman, kindly, 'but you must realise, Shelley was a very great artist—a free spirit and a philosopher. He was not quite like other men. That was part of his greatness.'

I could see she wanted that to be the end of it, but I had the light of battle in my eyes now. I wasn't Mother's daughter for nothing.

'Does that mean that if I can write poetry like this it doesn't matter if I keep my promises then?' I said.

Mrs Freeman's face wore a slight frown of irritation.

'Melissa,' she said patiently, 'Shelley was a very young man, and you are very young. You still have a great deal to learn. Now, how about the rest of the class? What do you think of the poem we have just been reading? Shirley?'

Shirley looked up from the complicated doodle she was perfecting in her notebook. She cleared her throat.

'It's ... it's ... it's got some good description in it ...' she ventured wildly.

'Norma?' said Mrs Freeman coldly.

'I don't know, really,' said Norma helplessly. 'It's a bit long and complicated. Perhaps he would have been better to write a proper story.'

Mrs Freeman drew a long, deep breath, and let it go in a sigh of discouragement. 'Let's leave it there for today,' she said, in a flat sort of voice. 'You can take down your homework in the last ten minutes. I will write the title for your essay on the board. Please have the plan ready for the next lesson. It may help you to read the introductory note to *Lyrical Ballads*, which starts after the foreword and the preface.'

I felt mean, somehow, as though I had squashed some-thing precious for her. She had been so absorbed in the poem. It was like Mary at the breakfast table, the sparkle in her eyes extinguished by our thoughtless laughter. I felt horrid inside, guilty. It must be rotten to be a teacher sometimes, to face a blank sea of faces, resisting you. It was as though we weren't people for the teachers, and they weren't people for us. Worse than enemies. *Strangers.* And yet ... and yet the poem *was* silly, and dishonest too, somehow. A lot of words without truth or goodness behind them ... I wrote down the homework, glad of the end of the day, but the lesson left a sour taste in my mouth. I wished I'd never said anything in the first place.

I waited for Therese after school and we walked slowly up the hill together. There was something kind and sensible about Therese that always made life seem safe and normal again, when fear or questioning or trouble invaded me. Even Therese looked gloomy today, though.

'Lilian did copy my essay,' she said, as we plodded up the hill. 'Mrs Freeman was cross about it, and told her off in class. Lilian won't speak to me at all, now.'

'*She* won't speak to *you*! It ought to be the other way round!'

Therese shook her head. 'She's my friend,' she said sadly, 'but come on 'lissa! Mary will be waiting for her birthday tea! Let's hurry up.'

It was a new idea to me that you could go on being someone's friend even when they'd done something awful to you, even when you felt as though you didn't like them any more. I quickened my pace to match Therese's. Lilian didn't seem worth it to me.

As we reached the gate, the door flew open, and Mary's eager, radiant face met us. 'Come and see my cake!' she cried. 'It says "Mary" and there are flowers and candles!'

It was a beautiful birthday cake, iced white with pink rose-buds. Six of the rose-buds on the top had little candles stuck in them, and Mary's name was written across the middle in pale green icing.

The birthday tea was wonderful, with crisps and tiny

sausages, little cubes of cheese and grapes and three kinds of sandwiches, brandy-snaps filled with whipped cream, and a huge lemon meringue pie as well as the cake. There was a big jug of Mother's home-made lemonade to wash it all down.

We ate every crumb, and drank every drop, but before we cut up the cake we lit the candles and sang 'Happy Birthday' to Mary, and she blew out all her candles in one go, with a bit of help from Cecily. After tea, the little ones went out to play in the garden, pink and sticky and content.

Therese and I helped Mother clear away the tea things before we did our homework. As Therese went down the step into the kitchen, carrying the big blue and white jug that held the lemonade, she missed her footing, and the jug shot from her hands and smashed into a thousand pieces on the tiled floor. There was a horrified silence, and Therese looked at Mother with pink cheeks and shocked eyes full of tears.

'It was an accident,' said Mother resignedly. 'Get the brush and dustpan, Therese, and sweep it up. Get every little bit, now, because Cecily runs about barefoot in this warm weather.'

Therese swept up all the pieces, and took them, well wrapped in newspaper, to the dustbin.

'It was my favourite jug,' said Mother sadly, as Therese went out of earshot, round the corner of the house, 'but there's nothing to be gained by shouting at her. Things just fly out of her hands. I have to say to myself, "She's like Brother Theo, she doesn't do it on purpose, don't be cross."'

My ears pricked up at this. 'Like who? Is it a story? Who was Brother Theo?'

'Yes, there's a story. At bedtime I'll tell you.' Therese came in from the garden, looking miserable. 'I am sorry, Mother. It was your favourite jug.'

'Darling, it couldn't be helped. Come on now and do your homework, while I wash up these things.'

I hurried through my maths homework, uneasily aware of having done some very shaky calculations, and did the reading and essay plan Mrs Freeman had asked for. The little ones came in from the garden for their baths as I was writing, and I could hear them in the bathroom, arguing about whose turn it was to sit on the plug, and Mother's tired voice growing impatient. I finished off my work quickly, and went to help her towel them dry and shepherd them up to the bedroom.

They played their game of trumpeting elephants and scuttling mice, and said their prayers, and then Mary and Beth wriggled into their beds while Cecily curled up on Mother's lap, squeaking softly, 'Weakness! Weakness!' as Mother stroked her hair.

At last the day was over. The sunset had blazed its last splendid banners and subsided to a dusky crimson afterglow. I drew the curtains on it, and lit the candle.

'You said there was a story, Mother,' I said, unable to contain myself any longer. 'You said there was at teatime; about Brother Theo. Are you going to tell us now? Is it—'

'Hush,' said Mother. 'You're filling the air with excitement. It's calm and quiet we need for a story. Yes, I'll tell you about Brother Theo; when you're ready to listen.'

We all settled down and waited, and into the silence Cecily began to sing in her high reedy voice:

> 'Free blind mice, free blind mice,
> See how they run, see how they run,
> They all run after the farmer's wife
> And cut her up with a carving knife ...'

'Hush now,' laughed Mother. 'Listen to the story. Here, put your thumb in your mouth. That's better.' Cecily cuddled in close to Mother, and a vacant, drowsy look came into her eyes as she sucked her thumb, held warm and close in the candle-light. Beth yawned a huge yawn.

'I am six now,' said Mary. 'I am a big girl. I have had a lovely day.'

'Have you, Mary?' said Mother, pleased. 'I'm glad it was a nice birthday. Snuggle down now.'

'Please, Mother,' I ventured.

'Ssh,' she said.

Brother Theodore was a novice at the Abbey of St Alcuin. He was always in trouble; he'd been in trouble all his life. It wasn't really his fault. His father had been telling him to take that look off his face ever since he could remember, but try as he might, he'd never been able to reassemble his features to suit him, and he continually aggravated and disappointed his father in a thousand other ways, too. He was slow and dreamy and inattentive, a forgetter of messages and a bodger of errands. He wanted to join in the games that the other children played, but he couldn't throw straight, and he couldn't catch a ball, nor could he run without tripping on his own feet, which were large and clumsy like the rest of him. When he was seven years old, he went to learn his letters, along with the other lads of his village, under the tuition of Father Marcus, the parish priest, but he was a poor pupil, never knowing what he had been asked to do, though his work was good enough when he did it. Taken all round, he was a child born to get under the skin of authority and irritate, and whippings and scoldings were his daily fare. Things didn't improve much when, on his thirteenth birthday, his father apprenticed him to the iron-fisted, sullen-faced village blacksmith, to learn a trade and make his way in the world. From his new master, as from his father and his teacher, he attracted nothing but beatings and derision, for the blacksmith was a surly and impatient man with neither imagination nor kindness to spare for his gangling and butter-fingered apprentice, whose incompetence was pushed to ridiculous lengths by his fear.

The one source of comfort and loving-kindness in the poor boy's life was his grandmother: a dear, wise, gentle old lady to whom he brought all his tears and his troubles from his babyhood until she died, when he was fifteen. She had been a devout woman, and from her he had learned in early childhood to love the Eucharist and to pray and to trust to God's goodness in spite of adversity. Her death reverberated in shock waves through his loneliness, and having no one else now in whom to confide, he clung in prayer to Christ crucified, and began more and more to long for the monastic life of prayer and service lived to God's glory.

Just after his eighteenth birthday, already world-weary, sad and sporting a black eye which was his parting gift from his father—who bitterly resented the waste of the money he had laid out on his son's apprenticeship— the young man entered the community of Benedictines at St Alcuin's. He came as much in the mood of a man seeking sanctuary as anything else, though there burned somewhere within him a small flame of hope that here, if anywhere, he would find acceptance and brotherhood, a place to belong. His name had rung in his ears like a clap of thunder in the mouths of irate parents and teachers until he was glad to hear the last of it when he made his novitiate vows and was clothed in the habit of the order, and tonsured, and given his new name which was Brother Theodore. He began his new life churning with mixed emotions: lingering grief for his grandmother, a sense of shame at his inability to succeed at anything, all mixed with a passionate longing to serve God well and to be a good monk. But for all his good intentions, here, too, he was always in trouble.

Father Matthew avowed that Theodore was the only novice who could slam a door opening it as well as shutting it. He was almost always late for his lessons, and sometimes for the Office too, however hard he tried to be in the right place at the right time. His habit was stained, torn and patched, and his hair around the tonsure looked like a crow's nest. He dreaded the days when it was his turn to wait on the brothers at table, in case a pewter plate should slip from his fingers and fall with a crash, causing the reader to lose his place and the silent monks to smile or glare according to temperament; or lest the pitcher should slip in his hands and he should splash water into someone's soup.

Poor Brother Theo. He was a thorn in Father Matthew's side; Father Matthew being neat and careful in all he did, and tidy and well groomed to the point of suavity. Father Matthew found Theodore exasperating beyond what his patience could endure, and berated him daily for his carelessness and clumsiness. He was determined to mould even this unpromising specimen of a novice into the quiet, unobtrusive, recollected character which was the monastic ideal; by exhortation, by penance, and occasionally even by the rod.

Theodore saw his hopes of a new beginning turn to ashes in the miserable discovery that even men who had given their whole lives to follow Christ could be irritable, sharp-tongued and hasty.

In spite of this sad realisation, life was not all misery, for among his habitual diet of failure and disgrace, Theo found in the monastery three places of refuge—sources of comfort and even of delight. The first was the scriptorium, for here, astonishingly, he proved to have an uncommon talent in the art of manuscript illumination, and a fair hand as a copyist, producing work of elegance and beauty.

He also discovered that he was musically gifted and could express in composition the same exquisite harmony and balance that showed in his manuscript work but was so disastrously lacking in all other areas of his life. So his second place of refuge was with the precentor, Brother Gilbert, with whom he spent time working on new settings for the Mass and the psalms and canticles, harmonising his clear and pleasant tenor with Brother Gilbert's baritone. Brother Gilbert treated him with friendship and respect—respect well-deserved too—and for this Theodore was grateful indeed. His family was one where there was neither interest nor pleasure in music or art, and these subjects were a new experience for him. Brother Gilbert and Brother Clement who oversaw the library and scriptorium noticed with interest that as Theodore was able to forget his self-consciousness and lose himself in the creative work he loved, so his clumsiness dropped away from him; and with ink and brush and pen and parchment he was deft and precise in all he did. They made no comment, but being artists themselves they understood, as Father Matthew did not, Brother Theodore's temperament.

Theo's third bolt-hole was the abbot's lodging, for he was often required by Father Peregrine to copy borrowed manuscripts for the abbey library, or to write at Peregrine's dictation now that his own hands served no longer for more than writing brief letters of an informal nature. It was a relief to find in Father Peregrine someone more clumsy even than himself and even more likely than he to spill food on its way to his mouth, or send a stream of ale shooting over the edge of a mug instead of safely into the middle of it. Neither did Father Peregrine glare at him, or wither him with icy sarcasm when the door handle slipped out of his nerveless fingers and the door crashed shut behind him. On the contrary, he treated him with unfailing gentleness and courtesy, and Brother Theodore found himself more relaxed and less clumsy as a consequence in Father Peregrine's company than with anyone else.

It had been some while now since Brother Theo had had the opportunity to do any copying or illuminating, or to make any music. It was the time for the hay harvest, and all able-bodied brothers who could possibly be spared from their usual work had been helping with the harvest, from the reaping until it was safely gathered and stacked, the barns filled against the lean months of winter. It had been a good year, with a warm, wet spring and dry breezy weather for the time of the harvest, so the whole community had sweated to get the hay in before the weather should break. The harvest was in now, and none too soon, for the heavy, stifling heat threatened thunder and rain.

With the barns full, the daily routine could be resumed. On the last day of the harvest, the brothers gathered in the community room after supper, weary and happy to relax for an hour before Compline.

Father Chad leaned back against the wall with a comfortable sigh, stretching his legs out before him. 'Your novices will welcome a day's rest after the work they've put in this week, Brother,' he remarked peacefully to Father Matthew, who sat beside him on the bench.

'Rest?' said Father Matthew in surprise. 'No, we shall be back to work as usual tomorrow. The lot I have at the moment are so slow with their Greek we could ill afford the week we've lost.'

Father Chad looked at him in disbelief. 'Matthew, you're jesting! They always have a day off after the harvest! Well, that is to say, when I was in the novitiate under Father Lucanus, we did. ...'

There was a slightly chilly pause. 'That possibly accounts for your difficulties with New Testament Greek, Father Prior,' said Father Matthew with calm disdain.

Father Chad, chastened, and unable to deny this deficiency, had no more to say.

The weary young men were back to work at half-past six on the following morning, with barely time beforehand to swallow their dry bread and water on which they broke their fast after the first Mass. Having kept them at their study of Greek for the better part of the morning, Father Matthew rather grudgingly gave them the three-quarters of an hour that remained after the community chapter meeting and before the midday Office of Sext for their own private reading and meditation.

Brother Theodore went up to his cell armed with a copy of Boethius' *De Trinitate* and the *Dialogues* of St Gregory. It was warm, almost hot, in his cell on this lazy summer day, and Theo could scarcely keep his eyes open as he read, his body still pleasantly aching and fatigued from the week's labour in the fields.

In the end, he laid his head on his arms ('I'll just close my eyes for one minute,' he said to himself) and slept as he sat: deep, satisfying sleep.

He awoke with a start, and listened. How long had he been sleeping? There was not a sound, nobody about. He dashed down the stairs to the chapel, paused warily outside the door and listened. They were already singing the *Kyrie Eleison*; that meant the Office was almost finished. He groaned inwardly. If he went in now, he would have to stand by himself in the place of disgrace reserved for latecomers, for the third time this week. Then would follow a cutting rebuke from Father Matthew, and kneeling to confess his fault before the abbot, to be given yet another penance.

Theodore's courage failed him. Already this week he had been in trouble for breaking a mug, for coming late to the Office and to instruction, for knocking over a stool with a terrible crash, and for singing during the Great Silence after Compline. He hadn't even realised he was singing! A new tune for the Magnificat was forming in his head, and he had sung softly without realising it as the phrases came together. Father Matthew, overhearing, had hissed in his ear, 'For shame, Brother Theodore,' and scowled at him frostily. He had been loaded with rebukes and penances and admonition until he was weary of life and of himself.

He turned away from the chapel door and plodded back up to his cell, where he sat down on his bed and stared gloomily at the crucifix on the wall, wondering what to do next. 'Lord have mercy,' he said wistfully, and then, 'Oh, God,' and sighed, and waited.

Before long the Office was ended, and he could hear the distant sounds of the brothers making their way to the refectory for the midday meal. Should he go down and slip in among them, in the hope that Father Matthew had not noticed his absence in the chapel? Not a chance. Better to go now to the scriptorium and begin his afternoon work and hope to avoid Father Matthew altogether, at least until the evening.

So Theo went to the scriptorium, sat down in his study alcove and looked at the page from the Book of Hours he was illuminating. He began to feel more cheerful at once, and was soon absorbed in his work, lost in concentration until the bell sounded for None, the afternoon Office. As soon as he heard the bell, he laid his work aside, determined for once to be on time, and bounded down the stairs to collide forcibly with Father Matthew at the foot of them, nearly knocking the wind out of the novice master's body.

Father Matthew looked at him with the expression of a man using extreme self-control. Brother Theodore began miserably to apologise, but Father Matthew cut him short. 'You were not in your place at the midday meal, Brother, nor were you present for the Office. Have you any explanation?'

'O God, O God,' thought Theodore. 'Now what?' Then it was as though all of a sudden something snapped inside him, and he heard himself saying, 'Father Abbot needed me to do some copying work for him, Father.'

'And he detained you through the Office and the midday meal?' asked Father Matthew in surprise.

'Yes, Father.'

'That's not like him,' said Father Matthew, with a puzzled frown.

'It was urgent, Father. He has a manuscript on loan that he wishes to copy before it is returned.'

'Very well, Brother,' said Father Matthew. 'It's odd, though. He usually lets me know if he has to keep one of the novices from their instruction or from the Office. It must have slipped his mind. Anyway, make haste now, or we shall be late. You'd better get yourself something to eat afterwards; you must be hungry.'

'Thank you, Father,' mumbled Brother Theo wretchedly, and followed his superior into the church.

It was in the peaceful hour after supper and before Compline that Father Matthew encountered Father Peregrine in the cloister.

'I would be grateful, Father, if you would remember to tell me when you require Brother Theodore to work for you,' he said, in tones of mild disapproval. 'He has already been in trouble almost continually this month, and I am having to watch him strictly. Today he was missing from both the midday Office and the midday meal, but when I took him to task over it, I find he was detained by yourself. Father, it is difficult enough to try to teach him discipline. If I don't know where he is it becomes impossible.'

Peregrine's eyebrows shot up in surprise, and he blinked at Father Matthew. Then he said, 'What are the things he has been in trouble for?'

'Father, the list is endless. He is careless, he is clumsy, he is late, he is noisy, he breaks things, he loses things; his behaviour is undisciplined in the extreme—why, last night I caught him singing during the Great Silence.'

'Singing, you say?' said Father Peregrine. 'I would have thought he had precious little to sing about!'

'Exactly so, Father. I have done all I can. He has been rebuked, he has been given penance, I have admonished him repeatedly. I have even resorted to the scourge.'

'Yes, I can imagine,' said Father Peregrine thoughtfully, 'and it makes it more difficult for you when you don't know what he's up to, or where he is, of course. I am too often thoughtless and forgetful. I ask your pardon. I have some work outstanding that I need him for in the morning. Perhaps you would send him to me.'

'Of course, Father,' said Father Matthew, and their conversation ended there.

In the morning, Brother Theo, by a great effort, managed to be in the right place at the right time, doing the right thing, and arrived for the morning novitiate instruction feeling cautiously optimistic, to be greeted by Father Matthew saying frigidly, 'Father Abbot requires you this morning, Brother Theodore. You are excused from your lessons.'

Theodore's mouth went dry as he received the summons, and his heart thumped as he trailed across the courtyard to the abbot's house. Did Father Peregrine know? He could not tell from the way Father Matthew had spoken. It was very possible that the novice master would mention his absence from Office and the midday meal, and then of course, Father Peregrine would have exposed his lie.

Reluctantly, Theo raised his hand and knocked at Peregrine's door, which stood ajar. *'Benedicite!'* called a cheerful voice from within, and Theodore entered and forced himself to look his abbot in the face.

'Good day, Brother,' said Peregrine with a friendly smile. 'I expect Father Matthew told you, I have some illumination work I need done. It is only a text for Master Goodwin from the village. He wants it for his daughter as a present for her child's baptism.'

Theodore stared at him, dizzy with relief. He didn't know! By some miracle, Father Matthew had not asked him about yesterday. With luck he would never find out and Theo would be safe!

'Yes, of course, Father,' he said and walked to the scribe's desk in the corner by the window, where parchment and inks, brushes and pens lay ready for him.

Father Peregrine stood by his own table, selecting a book from a pile that lay there.

'What is the text, Father?' asked Theodore.

'The text?' said Peregrine absently. 'Oh, it's from the Book of Proverbs, chapter twelve and verse twenty-two: *Abominatio est Domino labia mendacia: qui autem fideliter agunt placent ei.'*

'The Lord detests lying lips,' translated Theodore slowly, 'but he delights in men who are truthful.'

He stood and looked at Father Peregrine, but he was busy with his pile of books, his back turned to him. Did he know? It was a very strange verse to choose for a child's baptismal greeting. Theodore felt that familiar, horrible sinking feeling in the pit of his stomach. What now? Should he just write out the text and say nothing? *Could* he sit there all morning, carefully writing and illuminating such words, without owning up to his own lie?

Father Peregrine turned and looked at him enquiringly. 'Is something the matter, Brother?'

Did he know? Theodore couldn't tell. He loved this man, who had always treated him so gently and so courteously, and the thought of losing his respect was unbearable. To be clumsy and careless was bad enough in a monk, but to be a liar was despicable. But if he knew ... if he knew and Theodore said nothing, he would be in even deeper disgrace than if he didn't know and Theodore told him. And if he didn't know, did not God know anyway? And what was the point in trying to please men, when you had done the thing God detested, and told a lie?

Slowly, Brother Theodore knelt. 'Father, I ... I told a lie,' he said. 'I fell asleep yesterday morning, and didn't wake up until the midday Office was nearly over. I didn't go into the chapel. I told Father Matthew ...' Theodore struggled to keep his voice firm as he spoke. To his shame, he felt a hot tear escape from his eye. Father Peregrine waited and said nothing. 'I said you had kept me here doing some copying work for you,' finished Theodore bleakly. 'I'm sorry.' He clenched his teeth and stiffened his face against the tears. He had not known how much the abbot's friendship had fed his hungry soul until now he had lost it.

'God forgives you, my son, and so do I,' Father Peregrine said gently. 'Come and sit down and tell me about this, Theo.'

When Theodore raised his eyes, he was greeted by a kindly smile. All his life he had been used to steeling himself against rebuke and censure, but the unaccustomed kindness was too much for him, and he buried his face in his hands and sobbed like a child. Father Peregrine sat down on the scribe's stool beside him and waited for the storm to pass.

'God forgive us, we must almost have broken him, poor lad,' he thought as he looked on the bowed body, shaking in anguished weeping. He thought of St Benedict's recommendation in the Rule, that the abbot should remember his own frailty and have a care not to break the bruised reed, or destroy the pot in his zeal to remove the rust. 'The abbot in this monastery wouldn't get a chance to break the bruised reed, if he wanted to,' he thought. 'Father Matthew's in there before me, trampling on it in his tactless clogs. The scourge, indeed! Oh, poor lad, you have suffered. God help me now to find the right words and bring some healing there.'

Theodore, who never had his handkerchief, scrubbed at his eyes with his knuckles, and wiped his nose on his sleeve. Father Peregrine gave him his own handkerchief, and Theodore blew his nose noisily, and raised his woebegone face to look at him.

Peregrine burst out laughing. 'Oh, Brother, it's not so bad,' he said. 'Get up off the floor, man, and tell me what's been going on.'

Theodore told him everything. Simply, and without defending himself, he poured out his pain. He told him about the misery of his boyhood, his hope of a new life on entering the community, then the lateness and breakages and the slamming of doors, his inability to please Father Matthew. Hopelessly he explained how he had tried and struggled and failed, and finally his courage had failed him.

Peregrine listened without a word. Finally he said: 'Father Matthew tells me you are careless and clumsy.'

'He tells me it, too,' said Theodore miserably, 'and it's true. I am.'

'Brother Theodore, there is no one in this community with so fair a hand as yours or such a gift for illumination. I have never known you mar your work or overlook a mistake. I know that if I ask you to produce a document for me, it will be legible, beautiful and accurate. I have *never* known you be either clumsy or careless in your work. On the contrary, you make it beautiful with both artistry and conscientiousness.'

Theo gazed at the floor, dumb and embarrassed in his happiness. The words were like ointment on a wound. It had always been impressed upon him that work well done was no more than his duty, and though his work had always been in demand, it had never before been praised. Father Matthew felt that his soul was imperilled enough without giving him cause to be conceited.

'Now then, get up off the floor, my friend, and get to work on this text. Perhaps Master Goodwin would prefer something a little less menacing. Try Psalm 103 verses thirteen and fourteen: *Quomodo miseratur pater filiorum, miseratus est Dominus, timentibus se: Quoniam ipse cognovit figmentum nostrum, recordatus est quoniem pulvis sumus.*'

'As a father has compassion on his children,' said Theodore, 'so the Lord has compassion on those who fear him; for he knows how we are formed, he remembers that we are dust.' He got to his feet, but then his heart sank again as an unpleasant thought crossed his mind. 'Father, I suppose . . . should I tell Father Matthew about the lie I told, and confess it at community chapter?'

Father Peregrine sat looking up at him. His eyes were twinkling. 'Brother,' he said, 'from all I hear, Father Matthew has been zealous enough at pruning your unfruitful branches for one week. You have confessed your sin. It is done with. Put it behind you and get on with your work.'

Brother Theodore made that text a work of art. Just at the end of it where it said, 'He remembers that we are dust,' he painted a little lark, emblem of the soul of man, rising up out of the dust in song.

Mother got up from her chair and carefully carried the

sleeping Cecily to her bed. 'Sleep well, little Goldenhair,' she said softly, as she tucked her in.

'I like Brother Theo,' murmured Beth's drowsy voice, 'but not Brother Matthew. Brother Matthew is a baddy.'

'Father Matthew,' corrected Mother. 'Father, because he was a priest. Don't you like him, little mouse? He was a very good monk, though.'

'He wasn't kind. Christians should be kind.'

'That's right, my love. Perhaps he was trying too hard. Perhaps he was thinking so hard about being good that he forgot to think about being kind.'

'Well, anyway, I don't like him,' said Beth conclusively.

'That's because you like the rascals! You like Brother Tom best, don't you, because he was a mischief. Enough of that now, though. Snuggle down to sleep. Melissa, are you staying here or coming down for a while?'

'I'll come down,' I decided.

'Me too!' said Beth.

'Ssh, quiet, Beth, you'll wake Mary and Cecily. No, darling, you must stay in bed now. Melissa is a big girl, it's not her bed time quite, but she'll be up soon. Night-night now. I'll leave the door open, and you won't feel lonely.'

Mother blew out the candle, and we went downstairs.

VII
TOO MANY COOKS

Beth and Cecily and I used to get the most miserable colds as children; I can still remember the feeling. My nose would be blocked, all my sinuses throbbing painfully. The area under my nose would be sore with rubbing against my hanky; my lips would be cracked and dry from breathing through my mouth; my eyes would run and my head feel though it was full of porridge, thick and hot.

The season of colds, which ran all the way through to the end of February, started in November, when the magical, golden enchantment of autumn days (the wine of the seasons, when the year held its breath at the approach of frost and fire) turned into the raw damp of the back-end of the year, clogging leaves packed underfoot and chilling fog pervading everything. If I had to draw a picture of November, I think I would draw an old man in a grey macintosh, blowing his nose. Even the smoky delights of fireworks and baked potatoes on bonfire night do no more than hold off the depression of those creeping fingers of darkness and cold.

I turned fifteen at the end of October and had no sooner celebrated my birthday than the first of November found me flushed with fever and thick with catarrh. I moped and sweated under a mound of blankets in our frosty bedroom for a day, and snuffled and dozed through a delirious night, then by the morning the fever had subsided, and I was left feeling weak and fractious with the thick-headed, mouth-breathing, runny-eyed misery of a streaming cold.

When the others had gone to school, Mother lit a fire for me to sit by and made a nest for me on the sofa. She gave me hot elderberry cordial to drink, and made me inhale steam from a great enamel jug of friar's balsam dissolved in boiling water. I began to feel more cheerful, enjoying the luxury of being pampered and waited on, and I was looking forward to the afternoon, when Cecily, who had so far escaped my cold, was to go shopping with Grandma and I would have the precious treat of Mother's company all to myself for a whole afternoon.

I think Mother was longing as much as I was for an afternoon without Cecily. I had been short-tempered and irritable all week, and Cecily was like a simmering volcano at the best of times. Feeling too unwell to summon the patience and consideration she needed, I had fallen out with her before breakfast. She was ready to pick a fight with anyone by lunchtime.

Mother's patience was wearing thin too, but she managed to humour Cecily into eating her lunch, a thick vegetable soup with hot brown rolls and creamy butter that I could not taste. Then Mother swathed Cecily in her brightly-coloured scarf, gloves and hat, and buttoned her duffle coat on over the top, then stood her on a chair in the window to watch for Grandma. She stood very still, looking with great concentration at all the passers-by. 'That's not Grandma. That's not Grandma. That's not Grandma. Grandma!'

Grandma swept Cecily up into a big hug as she came in from the cold. 'There's my precious! Are you ready? Round the shops, then tea at Betty's and back in time for bed. All right, Mummy?'

'Sounds good to me,' said Mother with a smile. ''Bye 'bye Cecily. Have a lovely time. Here, you haven't got your shoes on!'

'And how are you, Melissa?' asked Grandma, as

Mother fastened on Cecily's shoes. 'Better for a day in bed I expect. I'll pick you up some of my herbal linctus from the pharmacy. That'll frighten any cold! See you later, then, ladies. Enjoy your afternoon.'

Mother waved goodbye to them from the door, then disappeared into the kitchen and returned five minutes later bearing a tray with two thick slices of fruit cake, a cup of coffee for herself, and some lemon and honey for me. She put another log on the fire and curled up in her armchair with her coffee cupped in her hands, looking into the flames.

'Peace,' she said happily. 'Oh, this is nice. It's nice when you feel peaceful inside, and you can curl up by the fire in a peaceful house. Too much racket in the house and it frays you at the edges a bit; but if you lose the peace on the inside of you, you could be in the quietest place on earth and your nerves would still jangle.'

I ate my fruit cake slowly. It is so difficult to eat when you have to breathe through your mouth. I felt quite exhausted by the time I'd finished. I drank the lemon and honey, and snuggled under my blanket on the mound of pillows Mother had provided.

'Tell me a story about Father Peregrine, Mother,' I said. She gazed into the fire, thinking, seeing, far away. Then she smiled.

'I never told you Brother Cormac's story, did I?' she asked.

'No!' I said. 'Tell me! He was one of the novices, wasn't he?'

He entered at about the same time as Brother Theodore, two years after Father Peregrine was attacked and beaten by his father's enemies. In those days, the novitiate lasted only a year before a monk was solemnly professed (nowadays it's a matter of years). Brother Tom was a novice longer than most—he entered just over two years before Cormac, but was with him in the novitiate for six months, too. At the time of this story, Brother Tom and Brother Francis had just made their solemn profession, and Brother Theodore, Brother Thaddeus and Brother Cormac were left in the novitiate, along with a young man called Gerard Plumley, who had not yet made his first vows and been given his new name.

Brother Cormac was an Irishman. He was a long, thin streak of a lad, with a wild tangle of black hair, and eyes as blue as speedwell. He had been an orphan since he was a tiny child. His mother and father died together in the seas off the coast of England, when the ship in which they were crossing the Irish Sea was hit by stormy weather, and foundered on the rocks. A wreck always drew a crowd: some to loot, some to watch and some to save lives. Under the grim sky and against the squalls of wind and rain, men dared the savage sea and brought to shore as many of the dead and the exhausted survivors as they could find. They found Cormac, only a baby then, about Cecily's age, clutching tightly to his drowned mother, terrified and half-drowned himself, and they left it to the gathering of women on the shore to separate the two.

They also saved from the wreck an Irish merchant who had made his home in York, and had been returning from a visit to his family in Ireland. The merchant recognised the scared waif, and was able to identify the child's father among the dead. The fishermen and the other local folk had mouths enough to feed at home, and nobody knew what to do with the orphaned child. He had fought and scratched and bitten his rescuers as they prised him free from his mother's body, but he sat quietly enough now, wrapped in a blanket on a bench in the inn which had opened its doors as a refuge.

The Irish merchant had no little ones of his own, and looking down at the blue eyes great with terror and shock in the child's blanched face, he took pity on him, and being full of gratitude to God for his own deliverance from the wild sea, he took the orphan home for his

wife to care for. This impulsive gesture of generosity
they often regretted, for the black-haired, blue-eyed elf
of a baby grew to be a wild, wayward, moody boy who
brought them more headaches than joy.

When he was eighteen, the earliest the monks could
take him, his jaded foster-parents steered him firmly in
the direction of the cloister, feeling that they had
done their fair share and more by giving houseroom to
this difficult charge. They thought of the monastery,
because one of his unreasonable habits was his flat
refusal, since he was eight years old, to eat anything of
flesh or fowl or fish or even eggs and milk. His dis-
traught foster-mother had thought at first he would
be ill without such wholesome food, but he proved
healthier than all the rest of the household on his dried
beans and vegetables; and besides, it was more trouble
than it was worth to try to dissuade him. Early conversa-
tions had gone something like this:

'Drink up your milk, my lad.'

'It is not my milk. It is for the calf.'

'Daisy the cow doesn't mind you drinking a drop, my
poppet.'

'It is not true. You have taken her calf away. She cries
for her calf.'

'She's only a beast, my pet. She won't fret long. Drink
up now.'

'It is the calf's milk. No.'

As he grew older, he would lecture his bewildered
foster-parents fiercely about their exploitation of God's
innocent creatures. His foster-father would look down at
the hunk of roast meat in his hand feeling a little queasy
as the piercing blue eyes fixed him with an accusing
stare, and his adopted son held forth passionately on the
freedom and grace of the running deer, the beauty and
serenity of the mother bird in her nest. In the end, what
with one thing and another, they'd had enough of him,
and knowing that all the monks, except the sick brothers
in the infirmary, abstained from eating the flesh of all

four-footed creatures, they felt it a reasonable com-
promise to send him there.

He was willing, though not enthusiastic, and realising
that the hospitality extended to his childhood need had
now run out, he saw no alternative but to comply with
their wishes and offer himself to serve and learn to love
God, in return for his bed and board in God's house. He
was fairly horrified to discover that there he would eat
what he was given and make no complaint, and he
submitted to this repulsive discipline with a bad grace
and a churning stomach. He did not make himself
popular in his first months with the community. He was
more than a little touchy and inclined to take himself
seriously and bear a grudge when anyone offended him.
In truth, he was more at peace with the animal kingdom
than with mankind or with himself.

The one person he did take to was Father Peregrine—
fortunately, since he was entering a life that would
involve vowing himself to total obedience to the abbot of
the community. When first he was brought to the abbot
by his foster-parents, he looked at the lean, hawk's face
with its savage scar, the still, twisted hands, and he felt
an unfamiliar stirring of compassion. Equally strange to
him was the uneasy feeling of inadequacy that grew in
him as the calm, shrewd eyes appraised him. Well used
to condemning other men, he was surprised by the
grudging but involuntary respect this maimed and
gentle monk's unassuming authority called forth in him.
As time went on, the grudging respect developed into a
fierce loyalty, and the incidents of the humble pie and
Brother Thaddeus' confession made their mark on him
and won his affection. He was grateful, too, that Father
Peregrine acknowledged his Irish origins in giving him
the name Cormac.

Thus it was that Brother Cormac began to love, who
had never loved; who had taken the tenderness that
should have been for brother and sister and mother and
father and given it instead to the birds and the beasts.

Because they could never be his kin, birds and beasts could never hurt him by being lost to him. So he began, awkwardly, to unfold.

In his first weeks in the abbey, Brother Cormac had been put to work in the scriptorium, but his restless and discontented spirit was unsuited to the disciplined and painstaking work. After his naming and clothing he was moved to work in the kitchens, which proved equally disastrous.

He and Brother Andrew took an instant dislike to each other, and the sparks flew at every encounter. Brother Andrew provoked him by making sarcastic comments to him if his work was badly done, and Cormac, though he was not openly insolent, yet managed to convey his dislike and contempt for the old man in every look and gesture. Brother Andrew further goaded him by insisting on mispronouncing his name and calling him 'Cormick', a minor yet infuriating pinprick, but the kind of gibe that was Brother Andrew's speciality.

'Cormac,' he would say, 'my name is Cormac.' But it didn't do any good.

In the end, Father Matthew moved him and sent him to work in the gardens and in the infirmary with Brother Edward, in the hope that the contemplative outdoor work of gardening and the care of the aged and the sick would between them bring to life a little gentleness and peace of mind in him.

One of his tasks in the infirmary was to help Brother Edward with the daily task of working and massaging Father Peregrine's stiff, crippled hands. Brother Edward thought those long, sensitive Irish fingers looked as if there could be skill in them if only they could be taught a little kindness. Besides this, Edward well knew the calming and tranquilising power that lay in aromatic oils, and he thought it would do Cormac good to work with them. As for Brother Cormac, he was only too relieved to be sent to work elsewhere than with Brother

Andrew, and determined he would never cross the old man's path or speak to him again if he could help it.

It was unfortunate for him that one day when it was his turn to serve at table, he knocked against Brother Andrew's arm, entirely accidentally, while pouring ale for one of the brothers. He caused Brother Andrew to spill the spoonful of vegetable stew he was holding, and splash gravy onto his habit. Andrew growled an irritable comment under his breath at Brother Cormac, who muttered sourly back at him. Father Peregrine's attention was caught by the exchange, and he saw the ill-tempered look that passed between them. He came later to find Brother Edward in the infirmary, and asked him: 'Would you say Brother Cormac is unhappy?'

'Unhappy?' echoed Brother Edward. 'Well I can't say I've ever seen him smile. Mind you, he's better since he's been away from Brother Andrew. They came close to blows, those two.'

Father Peregrine looked at him thoughtfully. 'And that is why Brother Cormac was moved away from the kitchens?' he asked.

'Oh, yes. Brother Andrew is a contrary old devil at the best of times, but it was as tense as a thunderstorm with the two of them together.'

'I didn't know. I was under the impression that Father Matthew felt the garden and infirmary work would be beneficial to Brother Cormac.'

'Well, that's true, but it was a matter of urgency to get him away from Brother Andrew. The atmosphere between them was poisonous.'

'He'll have to go back to the kitchen, then,' said Father Peregrine. 'No, it's no good, Brother,' he insisted in response to Edward's gesture of protest. 'There's no place in a monastic community for enmity and quarrelling. Somehow or other this must be resolved.'

He discussed the matter no further with Brother Edward, but went straight along to find Father Matthew. The day following, the novice master sent Brother

Cormac back to the kitchen to work, and Gerard replaced him in the garden and the infirmary.

Cormac was to continue with only one of his former tasks in connection with the infirmary. As they were so busy at that time of year (it was a raw, damp October) with bronchial coughs and feverish colds, he was told to keep on his daily job of working with Edward on Father Peregrine's hands, at least until the winter ailments had run their course. That this was mainly for his sake, to give him a restoring space in the midst of a difficult day, did not occur to him. He was merely appalled to find himself back in Brother Andrew's company.

A picture of sullen resentment, Brother Cormac presented himself in the kitchen after the morning instruction in the novitiate, to be greeted by the sarcastic old cook's 'Good morning, Brother Cormick. Better late than never. Would you prepare that pile of chicken livers yonder for the potted meat?'

'Cormac,' the young man replied through clenched teeth and turned to his work. His gorge rose in disgust at the sight of a pile of chicken livers sufficient to feed thirty monks, and he seethed with rage and resentment that Brother Andrew should have designated this work to him. Grimly, he set to work, and a long job it was, too.

It was well on into the morning, as things were getting busy towards lunchtime, that Father Peregrine came into the kitchen. The working area was not very spacious, and the staff were hard put to fit round each other as it was, so it was with a frown of annoyance that Brother Andrew broke off from his work to attend to the interruption.

'I'm sorry to trouble you, Brother Andrew,' Father Peregrine began courteously.

'I should think you are if you want your lunch on time,' was the reply he got.

The abbot looked a little taken aback, but persevered. 'Brother, I have come to beg a favour of you. You will probably know, it is difficult for me to maintain much movement in my hands, especially as I have no form of work for them in the course of my duties but a little writing. I wondered if I might come in here and work for a while each morning, so as to stretch them a little further?'

Brother Cormac looked up from the mangled pile of poultry offal. He was mildly surprised and puzzled. He knew—they all knew—that Father Peregrine hated to draw attention to the state of his hands. As he spoke now, his stiff formality sounded awkward and reluctant, as though he was wishing he could escape from Brother Andrew's irritated glare. There was something odd about it. Cormac looked at Brother Andrew, to see how he would take the suggestion.

Brother Andrew was staring at Father Peregrine in exasperation. His kitchen was crowded, and he had enough already to plan and arrange, but a request from the abbot was an order, however politely phrased. He had no choice but to obey. He didn't, however, have to be cheerful about it.

'Father, this is my busiest time of day. I cannot stop for conversation now. If you think it would be helpful to you, then come, but you'll have to keep yourself from under my feet. This kitchen is cramped enough already. I have no space for a lame man going to and fro. No doubt I could think of something to occupy you if you'll keep to a corner out of the way; but come tomorrow early, not now, because I'm run off my feet already.' And with this gracious speech, Brother Andrew turned back to his work and left Father Peregrine standing.

Cormac, watching, saw the muscle flex in Peregrine's cheek, and saw the imperious flash in his eye, saw him draw breath to reply but then he set his lips firmly, bowed his head, turned and limped out of the kitchen without a word. Recognising in that flash of the eye a spirit as fiery as his own, Cormac's proud heart paid unwilling tribute to a self-control he knew he could not match if he tried.

It was not that Brother Andrew was really unkind, just extraordinarily thoughtless, and not always able to make the distinction between plain speaking and plain rudeness. He did, at any rate, give careful thought to what tasks Father Peregrine could reasonably do in the kitchen, and took the trouble to discuss with him at some length the next morning just what he could and could not manage, ascertaining that although he could not cut anything very hard, like a turnip, or tough, like raw meat, and could not carry anything heavy unless he could hold it in his arm, he was able and willing to try any other tasks.

And try he did, humbly and largely unsuccessfully. Brother Andrew grew exasperated with him and did little to disguise the fact, annoyed as he was that this ridiculous whim of the abbot should have been visited on him.

Brother Michael, Brother Andrew's gentle and friendly assistant, did his best to help Father Peregrine with those things that were clearly beyond him. He watched him one morning, struggling to remove the flesh from a poultry carcass for a game pie. It had taken him long enough just to roll and fasten back the wide sleeves of his habit in order to tackle the messy task. He was up to his elbows in grease and once nearly had the whole dishful off the table onto the floor. He stopped and closed his eyes, wearily rubbing his hand across his brow, thereby transferring poultry fat to his face as well as his hands. He sighed, set to work again, and Brother Michael came and stood by him quietly, helping him to finish the job.

'Thank you, Brother,' he said, but Michael caught the note of humiliation mingled with polite appreciation.

Father Peregrine did his best to minimise the hindrance he caused by his slow lameness in the busy kitchen, and mainly occupied himself with jobs that involved standing still, or sitting at a work bench, out of the bustle of activity. Even so, he did get in the way sometimes. Things were always at their worst at about eleven o'clock, when the kitchen staff were scurrying to get the main meal of the day to the table promptly after the midday Office of Sext.

On one such busy morning, Brother Andrew stood at one of the tables making a rich pastry: he was using eggs and butter, and the rare luxury of wheat flour, for a party of visitors who were staying in the guest house. He stood with the flour and diced fat in front of him, and the basin of eggs to one side at the edge of the table. He worked swiftly and deftly with one eye to the incompetent way Cormac was chopping herbs for the stew a few feet away from him.

'Chop those finer, please, Brother Cormick,' said the Scottish voice sharply. 'You're working in my kitchen now, not shovelling in the garden.'

Cormac looked up at him with undisguised loathing, and continued his work without replying. Out of the corner of his eye, Brother Andrew was aware of a pot boiling too fast over the fire, and seeing on a quick glance round that everyone was fully occupied except Father Peregrine, who had just returned from his task of sorting through the onions in the store-room, he said, 'You might come and swing this pot off the fire for me, Father.'

Peregrine, hastening to be helpful, slipped on a little cube of butter that had fallen from the pastry-making as he passed Brother Andrew's table. He shot out his hand instinctively to the table to save himself from falling, but lost his balance and fell anyway. His hand caught the basin of eggs that stood at the edge of the table, and he sat down with a jarring thump on the floor, hitting the side of his head with sickening force on the edge of the table, the spilt eggs dripping down his neck and arm. He flushed crimson at the hastily suppressed guffaw of laughter that broke out from the two village lads working across the room.

'By all the saints!' exploded Brother Andrew. 'It's worse than having a child around the place! Yes, thank you, Brother Michael, clear it up if you would. John, fetch me six more eggs from the basket, and be quick about it. I'm behind as it is.'

Brother Michael helped Peregrine to his feet and cleared up the spilt egg from the floor quickly and without fuss. Peregrine stood a moment, his head still ringing from the impact of the table, the slime of broken eggs oozing uncomfortably down his neck and sleeve. Nobody took the slightest notice of him.

'I think I'd better go and find something clean to wear,' he mumbled.

Brother Andrew looked up briefly from his pastry-making. 'Aye, I should think you had, Father, you look like an egg nog.'

Peregrine bit his lip and limped to the door which led to the most direct path to the clothing room, where he could obtain a clean tunic and cowl from Brother Ambrose. It was a little door, opened by means of a little round knob, unlike the majority of the doors with their great cast-iron handles. He could not grasp the little knob properly, and he struggled to open the door and failed. He looked over his shoulder at the bustling kitchens he would have to cross to get to the other door, decided against it, and tried again, miserably, to turn the handle; without success. The cringing humiliation and despair of the early days of living with his disablement rose up in him again, and for a moment overwhelmed him. He stood helplessly, with his hand on the wretched little knob. He didn't know what to do. Brother Michael, seeing his predicament, came instantly to help him, and opened the door. Peregrine glanced once quickly at him and limped out.

Looking up from his work, Cormac saw Brother Michael go to open the door and return to his task of seasoning and thickening the stew with distress on his face. Cormac came across to put his now extremely finely chopped herbs into it, and Michael said quietly to him, 'Brother Andrew had almost reduced him to weeping. His mouth was trembling, Cormac. He had tears in his eyes.'

Cormac scowled. 'Tears! It's a punch on the nose the old scoundrel needs. Tears won't move him!' And he took himself off to the scullery to scrub pots violently on his own.

After that incident, the tension between Brother Cormac and Brother Andrew grew even worse. A storm was brewing. When Cormac came that afternoon to work on Father Peregrine's hands, his jaw was set with anger, and he hardly knew what he was doing. Peregrine winced under his handling, but Cormac's mind was on his own thoughts, and he did not see. As he left them to go to the novitiate chapter, Edward and Peregrine looked at each other expressively.

'There goes a miserable, angry young man!' said Brother Edward.

'I know. There's more tension in his hands than there is in mine,' said Father Peregrine ruefully. 'But let it be for now. This thing must be seen through somehow.'

It all exploded on the Thursday morning, three days later, about a month after Brother Cormac had come back to the kitchen and Father Peregrine had joined him there.

Peregrine was sitting at a table attempting to cut up a cooked beetroot with a vegetable knife. It was the middle of the morning, and Brother Cormac came in from his lessons in the novitiate.

'You're very late, Brother Cormick,' said Brother Andrew.

'Cormac. My lesson has only just finished,' muttered Cormac. 'What shall I do?'

'Slice this ox tongue finely and put it on a platter for the infirmary,' said Brother Andrew.

Cormac looked at the ox tongue and was nearly sick. His hand trembled as he worked, and he prayed silently, desperately, 'O God, please don't let me vomit. Help me. Please, please.'

An exasperated exclamation from the corner of the kitchen suddenly cut across his thoughts. Half of Father Peregrine's beetroot had escaped him and rolled onto

the floor. The other half lay in drunkenly cut slices on
the table in front of him. The knife had slipped, and he
had cut his finger. He addressed Brother Andrew
humbly: 'Brother, my hand is bleeding. I'm sorry to
trouble you, but have you a rag I could bind it with?'

'Aye. You'll find some in the cupboard yonder,' said
Brother Andrew, 'but pick up that beetroot off the floor,
or you'll be falling over that next.'

Peregrine obediently retrieved the fallen beetroot,
and then limped across the kitchen, his finger in his
mouth. Cormac, watching him, saw he had no hope of
managing the cupboard door, the crutch and the rags,
when blood ran down his finger every time he took it out
of his mouth. He moved to help him.

Deep inside Brother Andrew knew it was mean, even
though he was busy, to leave Father Peregrine to fend
for himself. He was justifying it by telling himself that if
Peregrine had come to learn to use his hands it was
better to let him do so, when he saw Cormac go to help
him. 'And where do you think you're going, Brother
Cormick?' he asked, acidly.

Cormac's self-control finally snapped. 'My name is
Cormac!' he bellowed, 'and I was going to help him,
which is more than you would, you ill-tempered, un-
charitable, miserable, sour old troll!' He said a lot
more besides, which was even less polite, and Brother
Andrew, bristling with fury, opened his mouth to reply.

Before he could do so, Father Peregrine spoke.
'Brother Cormac, that will not do,' he said firmly. 'You
will beg his pardon, please,'

Cormac stood, trembling with anger, glaring at
Brother Andrew.

'I said, my son, please beg his pardon.'

'I'm sorry,' Cormac muttered woodenly, still glaring,
still trembling.

'Brother Cormac, please look at me when I'm speaking
to you,' said Peregrine calmly. Cormac turned his head
slowly to look at him, the blue eyes still icy with rage,

hardly seeing him. 'Please beg his pardon properly,' said Peregrine.

'I said, I'm sorry,' ground out Cormac from between clenched teeth.

'It comes better from you on your knees, my son,' persisted Peregrine quietly.

The blue eyes blazed at him with their cold fire, and Cormac slowly shook his head. 'Kneel?' he said. 'To him? No.'

Brother Andrew again drew breath to speak, quivering in his indignation. Father Peregrine stopped his interruption with a peremptory gesture, without looking at him. His gaze still held Cormac's. 'Son, do it,' he said.

The moment of violent conflict that took place then in Cormac's soul nearly wrenched it out of orbit. Anger and rebellion and disgust at the self-abasement required of him boiled inside; but yet he had not forgotten the self-control and ability to humble himself that he had seen in Peregrine, and he knew instinctively that that was the stronger thing, stronger than anger, stronger than hate, stronger than Brother Andrew. He had a sudden intuition that if he could not kneel before his ill-mannered old adversary, it was he who would have lost the battle, not Brother Andrew, not Father Peregrine. It was the moment he made up his mind, late, that he really did want to be a monk. He knelt. The kitchen was utterly still, watching in fascination.

'I confess . . .' he said, gratingly.

'I think "humbly" is the word you're looking for,' said Father Peregrine quietly.

'I . . . humbly . . . confess,' said Cormac, shaking, dizzy with pent-up rage, 'my . . . fault . . . of disrespect . . . and . . . rudeness. I ask God's forgiveness and. . . .' He stopped, looking down at his hands, which were clenched into fists, the knuckles white. The saying of the next word seared him to the soul. He felt as though it cost him everything he had as he whispered, '. . . yours.'

He looked up, but it was Peregrine's face he sought,

not Andrew's. He was rewarded by the admiration and respect that shone in his abbot's eyes. Peregrine nodded at him, almost imperceptibly.

Brother Andrew cleared his throat, slightly shaken by the situation. There had been a moment when Cormac had looked almost mad, when Brother Andrew had realised he was more likely to get a black eye than an apology.

'God forgives you, my brother, and so do I,' he said as required, but the dry irony of his voice betrayed that it was the formula only, and his heart was not in it. So far as he could see, the rebellious and disobedient boy had been as defiant to his superior as he had been appallingly rude, and had had to be forced into submission to an extent that any other abbot would have had him whipped for. Only Father Peregrine, looking into those ice-blue eyes, had known quite well that neither he nor anyone would ever be able to make Cormac do anything: the lad's battle was with himself, and he had won it, too.

'Brother Cormac, I think it may be better if you go and help Brother Edward in the infirmary for the rest of the morning,' said Father Peregrine, and Cormac stood up, nodded his assent and was gone. The quiet hum of activity began again as the kitchen staff hastily took up their work.

'Brother Andrew, please will you come and see me one hour after the midday meal,' Father Peregrine said pleasantly. 'I'm sorry to have so delayed and hindered your work. I think I may have caused enough trouble for one morning. I'll leave you in peace.'

It was not long before the bell would be ringing for Sext, and Peregrine made his way slowly to the chapel. There was a fine mist of rain, and the winds blew in fitful gusts, driving dead leaves into little drifts against the foot of the stone walls. Inside the chapel, the air was damp, and the light dim. On the wooden stalls, there lay a rime of moisture. Winter was closing in. Peregrine sat in his stall, feeling suddenly cold and weary. He looked down at his hand. His finger was smarting, and he cautiously unclamped his thumb from where he had held it against the cut. The bleeding had ceased, but it stung. He sucked it, looking sightlessly ahead of him, his thoughts drifting.

Cormac ... Andrew ... he sighed and smiled, shaking his head. What a pair! A letter that must be written after lunch. Better eat in his own house, because he must be back from the infirmary in time to see Brother Andrew an hour after the meal ... *Brother Andrew* ... Peregrine's eyes focused on the great wooden crucifix that hung over the altar. 'What would you do with him?' he wondered. 'I have to resolve this somehow, my Lord. Help me to make him see. Poor Cormac, I can hardly blame him losing his temper. I've had to bite my own lip a time or two these past weeks. Dear Lord, he was angry. I thought he'd not obey me. Thought I'd pushed him too far. Brave lad. Brave, and very hard work. Help me to treat him right.' He gazed at the crucified Christ, the bowed head, the hands splayed back against the cross, pinned with great, cruel nails, and he shuddered. 'My God, what a price! Follow you? The thought makes me sick. Lead me, then, lead me. I haven't got what it takes to walk that path on my own.'

The bell began to ring for Sext, and the brothers were coming in silently to their places, their faces shadowed by their cowls, their sandalled feet whispering on the stone floor. 'Chad ... Ambrose ... Fidelis ... Theodore— Theodore! He's in good time, well done, lad ... John, Peter, Thomas, Edward, Cormac, Mark, Francis, Cyprian, Gilbert, Clement (must have a word with him about that new manuscript), Stephen, Martin, Paulinus—he's limping badly; his poor old knees are stiff and swollen in this weather. Matthew, Giles, Walafrid, Thaddeus, young Gerard, shaping up nicely, I think there is a vocation there, Dominic ... Denis and Prudentius both laid up with a racking cough, and Lucanus won't stir from the infirmary again now, dear old soul. No Andrew, no Michael, that's my fault, causing a commotion in the kitchens just before the meal. No one else late or absent, old Brother Basil slipping into his place, back from ringing the bell.'

'*Deus in adjutorium meum intende,*' rang out the cantor's chant.

Abbot Peregrine gave his mind to the Office.

Brother Cormac presented himself at the infirmary as instructed, and sought out Brother Edward, who was checking his supplies of medicine. 'Good morning, Brother, what brings you here? Remind me to ask Brother Walafrid for some more of his soothing brew for poor old Brother Denis. He's coughing fit to break himself apart.'

'Father Abbot sent me,' said Cormac cagily.

Brother Edward glanced at him sideways. 'Did he? Why ever did he do that?' he enquired innocently.

In spite of himself, Cormac was amused. For the first time ever that Brother Edward could recall, a brief flicker of a smile lit his face. Almost instantly, it clouded over again.

'I quarrelled with Brother Andrew,' he said. 'Father Peregrine cut his hand, and Brother Andrew wouldn't let me help him get a rag to bandage it. I lost my temper with him.'

Brother Edward turned to look fully at Cormac. He regarded him silently for a moment before he replied. Then, 'Brother,' he said, 'day by day you tend that man's hands with me. Have you not eyes to see the state of them? They are blistered with burns and sore with scalds and little cuts, and bruised too from those kitchen tasks he simply cannot manage.'

'Well, I know,' replied Cormac, 'but he said he needs to use them to keep them moving freely. I suppose he'll manage better in time.'

Brother Cormac was taken aback by the sudden flash of anger on Edward's kindly face. Edward stood, contemplating him, until Cormac began to feel uncomfortable.

'He would not wish me to say this,' said Edward slowly, at last, 'but somebody needs to tell you. He's not working in the kitchen for the sake of his hands. The damage done to those hands can't be put right by work; they're beyond repairing. Believe me, I know they are; it was I who struggled to save them when they were smashed and broken and bleeding; and every day as I do what I can to ease the discomfort in them, it breaks my heart that I had not the skill to do a better job. No, he came because he saw you and Brother Andrew had bad feeling between you and he wanted you to sort it out; but between your sulks and Andrew's ill humour he knew there would be trouble, and he thought he should be there to keep an eye on things. What else could he do? Stand in the corner with his mitre on, arms folded, tapping his foot, watching you sternly?'

Cormac looked at him, appalled. 'Are you saying,' he asked, horrified, 'that he doesn't need to be there for himself at all? That he came only for Brother Andrew and me?'

'That's about it, young man. You maybe thought, did you, that the abbot of a monastery has nothing better to do with his time than while away the morning in the kitchen, hindering the meal preparation?' Cormac just gazed at him, dumbly. 'Oh, but hark at me,' said Brother Edward repentantly, 'I sound as scathing as Brother Andrew, now; and there goes the bell for Sext and these chores not half finished. Never mind, lad. Come, let's go to chapel.'

The midday meal over, Father Peregrine came to the infirmary as usual, and Brother Cormac and Brother Edward sat in silence to work on his hands. Cormac took the right hand and Edward took the left. Brother Cormac looked attentively at that hand for the first time. Until now, he had been too full of his own problems to see properly beyond them. The cut from the morning, which never had been bandaged, was still open a little, and grubby, and getting slightly inflamed. It was on the side of the first joint of the second finger.

'That looks painful,' said Cormac.

'I had to write a letter,' replied Father Peregrine. 'The pen just catches it and makes it a bit sore.'

Cormac looked at him. 'He did it for me,' he thought.

'It's on your right hand,' he said. 'How did you come to cut your right hand?'

'My right hand was getting cramp trying to hold the knife, so I thought I'd try if I could do it better with the left. I learned to my cost that they may neither of them work, but I'm still a very right-handed man!'

Cormac straightened the fingers gently and examined the little burns, cuts and sore places. 'For me,' he thought, 'and not only that, but the sharp orders that made him look clumsy and foolish and in the way.' He remembered Brother Andrew's irritation: 'It's worse than having a child around the place!' and Brother Michael's distress: 'He had tears in his eyes.'

Cormac said nothing, but he gently salved the sore places, carefully disinfected and bandaged the cut, then worked over the whole hand as he'd been shown. This time he was seeing with his fingers, as Brother Edward had tried to teach him to do, finding the places where muscles were cramped and knotted, easing them out. When he had finished, he got to his feet and turned away without looking at Peregrine's face, and made himself busy putting away oils and salves and lint.

'Thank you,' said Father Peregrine quietly. 'Thank you for your healing love.'

Cormac looked at him a moment, then shook his head. Then, 'I'll be wanted back in the kitchen,' he said, and he left them.

'Whatever happened to him?' said Father Peregrine. 'Where on earth has this gentleness come from? Brother Edward, you've had a hand in this, I suspect.'

'I don't know,' replied Edward. 'I think it was more likely your hands.'

'Well, whatever it was, thank God for it. I couldn't have stood too many more mornings like this one. Now then, I must go and find Brother Andrew. Thank you for your care, Brother.'

He found Brother Andrew waiting for him in the abbot's house, ill at ease out of his own domain, looking older and less autocratic away from his little kingdom in the kitchen.

'Sit down, Brother, that's right. I'll come straight to the point. I know you have work to do, and so do I. This concerns Brother Cormac, as I expect you realise. To be blunt, Brother, you have treated him abominably. Your insensitivity and unimaginative dealing with him is shameful. I have never heard a monk speak with less courtesy and more rudeness than you do. You deliberately provoke him by miscalling his name, and that is inexcusable. Also, it is thoughtless and unkind to ask him to prepare meat unless it is absolutely necessary. You know well what a revolting task it is to him. Well? What have you to say?'

Brother Andrew sat rigidly still, looking down, mortified. Away from the pressure of work in the kitchen, away from the aggravation of Cormac's hostility and unwillingness, he saw his own behaviour in a different light.

'I have nothing to say,' he mumbled. 'What can I say?'

'You will confess your fault at chapter in the morning. From now on, this has to stop. If you cannot find it in your heart to love, you can at least keep a civil tongue in your head. Have you understood me?'

'Yes, Father.'

'Thank you. You can go.'

Brother Andrew forced himself to look at Peregrine and was startled to see nothing but gentleness and concern in the eyes that looked back at him, where he had expected cold rebuke.

'I'm sorry, Father,' he said humbly. 'Truly I didn't think about the meat, but for the rest, it's true what you say, I admit it. I'll try to mend my ways.'

Father Peregrine nodded and watched the old man with affection as he went on his way. 'He wants to mend his ways, Lord,' he prayed silently as Brother Andrew closed the door. 'He'll need your help, then. That the habits of a lifetime were so easily undone! But you can't help loving the peppery old codger. O Christ, be the bridge between them, stubborn men both and proud. It was a privilege to feel Cormac's gentleness, but if you could divert a crumb, just a crumb of it from me to Andrew, it would make life so much easier.' He sighed. 'And who am I, that I should be asking you of all people for an easy life? As you think best then Lord, but only, give me patience when my own runs out. ....'

Brother Cormac had gone from the infirmary to the kitchen, which was empty now in the quiet time after the meal. He sat on a stool by a work bench, thinking, for a long while. Hearing the door open, he looked up, and seeing Brother Andrew, stiffened at once against anticipated sarcasm and hostility.

'Brother Cormac, I was looking for you,' Andrew said. 'Father Abbot has just been speaking to me. Scolding me, really. He says I've treated you rudely and insensitively. He rebuked me for miscalling your name. Brother, I'm sorry. I truly didn't think when I asked you to cut up that ox tongue. I'm sorry about your name, Brother Cormac, and for all my rudeness, I am sorry.'

Cormac was stunned. He sat and looked at him for a moment, an anxious, contrite old man, unsure of his reception, not an ogre, not to be despised. He jumped off his stool and flung his arms impulsively around his enemy. It is hard to say which of them was more amazed by his action, 'Me too,' Cormac said as he hugged him, 'I'm sorry.'

'For pity's sake, Brother,' flustered Andrew, disentangling himself, 'calm yourself! Sit you down, for heaven's sake, you wild, unpredictable, Irish whirlwind. What's all this?'

He listened soberly as Cormac recounted what Edward had told him. 'You mean he came here, not for himself, but for us? Oh, Brother, I was never more ashamed of myself in my life. Whatever should we do?'

Cormac looked at him shyly. 'Make our peace?' he suggested, with a small grin, the second in one day.

From that day onwards, Brother Andrew and Brother Cormac were friends, and there grew between them a bond of affection and understanding which transformed the two touchy, hot-tempered, and—underneath it—lonely characters. Not that they were always polite to each other.

Father Peregrine was passing the kitchen six weeks later, at the busy time just before lunch. Brother Cormac was strolling down the corridor ahead of him, late for work, and entered the kitchen as Peregrine passed.

'Where the devil have you been, you good-for-nothing Irish rascal?' roared an indignant voice.

'I came the pretty way,' came the nonchalant reply.

Father Peregrine smiled and shook his head as he continued on his way.

Mother leaned forward on her chair and prodded the fire with the long brass poker. A shower of sparks flew up and the soft white ash fell in the grate. She put another log on. Gingerly, I blew my sore, hot nose.

'He always seemed to hurt himself, Mother.'

'Yes, I know what you mean, my love,' she said reflectively. 'I think there were two reasons for that. One was simply that a man with broken hands can't protect himself, or manage tools and things as well as we can. But also, it was because he wanted so much to be like Jesus, he wasn't afraid to put himself in the place where he was vulnerable to hurt.

'Oh, Melissa! Look at the time! There'll be nothing for tea if I don't get cracking! I shall have to go and meet Mary and Beth in half an hour, and they'll all be famished in this cold weather!' And she leapt to her feet and disappeared into the kitchen.

VIII
BEGINNING AGAIN

The year had rolled to its close. New Year's Eve was a night of tingling frost, the stars shining sharp and bright in a cloudless sky, the moon riding clear and lovely in the heavens.

Huddled in my dressing-gown and a woollen shawl, I stood in the garden with Therese and Mother and Daddy, waiting to welcome in the New Year. The little ones had gone to bed late, and were now tucked up fast asleep, clutching their new Christmas dollies. They were snuggled in under extra blankets, their mattresses pushed close together so they could keep each other warm. I was sleepy too but would not have missed the magic of this moment for anything.

In the morning, we would wake up to windows decorated with frost flowers, all the grass and skeletal bushes in the garden would be stiff with hoar frost. The end of my nose and the tops of my ears hurt in the biting cold. I breathed out into the midnight air, and in the moonlight the impressive, ghostly cloud looked like a dragon's breath.

Far away, but clear and sonorous on the cold, still air, the church clock began to chime midnight. Distant, but perfectly distinct, we counted the twelve strokes and then stood there a moment on the silent moonlit threshold of another year.

'Happy New Year!' Daddy's cheerful voice lifted the

moment from solemnity and awe to party-time. 'Come indoors, ladies! I have some hot mulled wine and some goodies for you.'

We sat and sipped and munched by the fire, the room lit by candles at Mother's pleading, instead of the electric light. After a while Daddy stretched and yawned. 'I'm for bed,' he said, in sleepy contentment.

'I'll follow you soon,' said Mother. 'Warm up the bed for me.'

He and Therese took the glasses and the plates out into the kitchen, and we could hear Daddy's heavy tread going slowly up the narrow stairs, and the chinking of glass and crockery as Therese washed up. We heard her fill the kettle for her hot-water bottle, and then shortly after, she put her head round the door to say goodnight.

'Goodnight, Therese,' said Mother. 'Thank you for washing up. Happy New Year.'

'Happy New Year. I'll put the hot-water bottle in your bed, 'lissa, when I'm warm, if you're not coming up straight away.'

I smiled my thanks, and we sat, watching the fire, Mother and I, listening to Therese's footsteps mounting the stairs. There was no sound but the ticking of the clock and the settling of the glowing logs.

'What are you thinking, Mother?' I said.

She stirred in her chair and sighed. 'It's a funny thing,' she said thoughtfully, looking with wide, faraway eyes into the low, red flames. 'The thing life is fullest of is the thing we find hardest to believe in. New beginnings. The incredible gift of a fresh start. Every new year. Every new day. Every new life. What wonderful gifts! And when we spoil things, and life goes all wrong, we feel dismayed, because we find it so hard to see that we can start again. God lets us share it too, you know. Only God can give life, it's true—make a new baby or a new year—but he gives us the power to give each other a new beginning, to forgive each other and make a fresh start when things go wrong.'

She fell silent, thinking, then she started to smile.
'That reminds me—yes, I hadn't thought of that for a
long time. Poor Brother Tom! Oh, that was a bad
evening ...'

She laughed, and I looked at her impatiently. Five
minutes ago I had thought I was sleepy, but I felt wide
awake now. 'Oh, come on, Mother, tell me, then! What
happened?'

She glanced up at the clock and hesitated.

'Oh, you've got to tell me now!' I cried. 'What about
Brother Tom? What happened?'

'Ssh, all right then, pipe down. I'll tell you the story.
Put another log on the fire, though, first.'

She watched me as I pushed the little apple log into
the heart of the fire, then she began.

It was the year of our Lord 1316. King Edward on the
throne, a year of tranquillity and kindly weather. The
month of June blazed with sunshine, and the brothers
got their hay in early. The elder trees were loaded with
blossom, promising delicious wines for the year following and a good crop of berries to soothe coughs and
colds in the autumn chills and mists. The summer continued fiercely hot and dry; the water in the well ran low
and the grass withered brown and dusty, but September
came with a mellow, lazy warmth, kindly mists in the
mornings and long, slow, dreamy afternoons.

Through the hot summer and on into the golden
September days, the old brothers whose last days were
spent in the peace of the infirmary were brought out to
sit and doze among the herbs in the physic garden, and
there they sunned themselves, lulled to drowsiness by
the hum of the bees and the fragrance of the herbs,
caressed by the almost imperceptible breeze.

Abbot Peregrine had ruled his flock at St Alcuin's
Abbey for twelve years now, and the brothers loved him
for his gentleness, humour and wisdom, and respected
him for the courage and strength that lay beneath. He

was in his fifty-seventh year now. The remains of his crisp, black curls were grey. All traces of youth's softness had gone now from his face, which left it more hawk-like and eager than ever. Age had done nothing, however, to dim his disconcerting grey eyes—they had lost none of their directness and urgent power.

Brother Cormac, Brother Theodore and Brother Thaddeus were all fully fledged, dignified monks now, and Gerard Plumley had become Brother Bernard, which Brother Tom said was a radical improvement. Tom himself was these days employed as the abbot's personal attendant. He helped Peregrine with the impossibilities of shaving and fastening his sandals and his belt, and he cleaned the abbot's house. He also waited at table for Peregrine when visitors came to the abbey, to cut his food and serve his guests with food and wine. Father Peregrine's maimed hands could not perform either of these tasks with any reliable outcome, and it was in any case the customary thing in those days for the abbot of a monastery to have at least one or two personal servants.

Brother Tom had been fully professed almost eight years now. He was just approaching his thirtieth birthday, the end of his tenth year in the community, but he was still not master of his irrepressible nature, and could be as undisciplined as a schoolboy in the company of Brother Francis, whose composed and urbane exterior hid a spirit as mischievous as Tom's own.

There was a new generation of novices—Brother Richard, Brother Damian, Brother Josephus, and Brother James, who had just had his clothing ceremony and was bursting with delight at being allowed to wear the habit of the order. The novitiate was still watched over by Father Matthew's stern and exacting authority, though he was feeling his age now.

In the kitchens, Brother Andrew still ruled, with the help of Brother Cormac and young Brother Damian. Brother Michael had gone to work with Brother John in the infirmary, where his thoughtfulness and gentleness did excellent service. Although Brother Edward was more than eighty years old now, and as light and wrinkled as a withered leaf, he was still officially the infirmarian. His heart and wind were still as sound as a bell, and his mind still sharp and clear, but his sight and hearing were growing dim, and he relied more and more on Brother John and Brother Michael in the infirmary work. In the afternoons he was allowed to drowse in the sun in the herb gardens outside the infirmary in the company of the other old men, of whom he was no longer the youngest.

On this particular day, Brother Edward was sitting with Brother Cyprian to keep an eye on him lest his usual peaceful docility should erupt into one of his occasional, unpredictable fits of eccentric behaviour. Brother Cyprian had for years been the porter of the abbey—a wise, discreet and kindly man, whose job had given him a wealth of insight into human nature—but he was very old now, toothless and senile and incontinent. Brother Martin had replaced him as porter, and Brother Cyprian now dreamed and wandered and slept, propped with pillows in his chair, his veined and freckled old hands resting on the woollen rug that Brother Michael had carefully tucked around him. The experience of a lifetime was not all lost, however, and from time to time he would interrupt his vacant staring and the rhythmic chewing of his gums, to narrow his eyes thoughtfully and utter with typical Yorkshire bluntness a surprisingly shrewd and observant comment about his brothers in the monastic life.

Father Peregrine had been to the infirmary for Brother John to exercise and massage his stiff, misshapen hands, and he stopped in the garden to talk to the old brothers, telling Brother Edward news he had just received of his daughter Melissa.

'Edward, she has another child, a baby boy. She says both she and the infant are thriving.'

Melissa had been married eight years to her wool merchant, Ranulf Langton, and they had recently moved to Yorkshire, where the fleeces of the abbey's flocks were renowned throughout Europe. Ranulf's business was prospering, they were comfortably and happily settled, and Melissa had just sent word to Father Peregrine of the birth of her fourth child, a boy, Benedict.

Peregrine glowed with pride as he spoke of her, and Brother Edward nodded and smiled obligingly as he heard the details of her letter lovingly recounted. They neither of them noticed Brother Cyprian's unfocused gaze sharpen until he was looking with close attention at Peregrine's face, disfigured and scarred but somehow beautiful with the joy of his love as he told Edward his happy news.

'I don't know what 'appened to thee,' interrupted Brother Cyprian suddenly, his red-rimmed old eyes looking acutely at Peregrine, taking in his scarred face and hands and the crutch he leaned on. 'Knocked all about by t' look o' thee. Eh, but tha was an aggravating, strutting peacock when tha came! Aye, smile! Go on, laugh if tha will, but 'tis true! Tha thought thyself a king on thy throne. Knocked thee off, did they? Aye, well, never mind, lad. Learned thee a bit o' sense, I can see that.'

He blinked the reptilian lids of his hooded old eyes and chuckled to himself. Father Peregrine stood looking at him, startled, amused and not sure how to respond, but the old man had retreated into his own world, chewing and gazing. Presently he slipped into a doze; and his mouth fell ajar as the toothless jaw slackened.

'Father—' Young Brother James' voice at his elbow claimed Peregrine's attention. 'There is a party of folk asking hospitality for the night whom Brother Martin thinks you would maybe wish to greet.'

Father Peregrine turned away from Brother Cyprian, still smiling.

'Did he give you a name?'

'Yes, Father, he bids me tell you it is Sir Geoffrey and Lady Agnes d'Ebassier.'

A shadow of weariness clouded Father Peregrine's face. The names were those of a wealthy Norman baron and his wife, landowners from just south of Yorkshire. They stayed from time to time at St Alcuin's to break the journey to Scotland, where Lady Agnes' brother-in-law owned some excellent hunting and fishing territory. Sir Geoffrey and his lady were deeply pious, good people, generous benefactors whose gifts were more than helpful to the finances of the abbey, but they were not easy guests. They liked to think of St Alcuin's as home from home and felt entitled to drop in unannounced at any time as their gifts of money to the brothers were so frequent and so large. This could be awkward at times, and besides this their keen consciousness of their own social standing and the rigid formality of their manners imposed a strain even on themselves. Father Peregrine found it exhausting. He sighed as he looked at Brother James. The joy of his letter and his amusement at Brother Cyprian had suddenly evaporated. He felt the first tightenings of his shoulders and neck that would develop inevitably into a thundering headache as the evening drew on.

'Thanks, Brother,' he said heavily. 'Yes, it would be right for me to make them welcome. Have they come with a great many servants?'

'Not so many as last time, Father. Six, only. My lady's personal maids, Sir Geoffrey's manservants and two grooms.'

'Six. I see. Very well then, see to it that their beasts are stabled and so forth, if that is not already done. My lord and lady will expect their servants to eat in the kitchens of the guest house. Would you arrange that? Thank you, Brother, I will come directly to my house to welcome them there when they are washed and rested.'

Brother James turned to go, but Father Peregrine

called him back 'Oh—Brother, if you will: when you go
into the kitchen would you ask Brother Cormac to put
me aside a bite of bread and cheese or some such thing?
Tell him I shall come for it before Vespers, because I
can eat next to nothing with company like this to dine.'

Brother James set off on his errand, and Father
Peregrine took refuge a little longer in the comfortable
gathering of old men in the herb garden, discussing
their ailments and reminiscing with Brother Edward.
But at last he could put it off no longer, and with a
sigh of resignation, he bid them farewell and limped
gloomily to his own dwelling to await his guests.

As he came through the narrow passage into the
cloister, he met with Brother Tom and Brother Francis,
who were carrying a wooden bedstead across from the
dormitory to the infirmary. Brother Fidelis had that
morning put a fork through his foot in the vegetable
garden, and there were too few beds to accommodate
him in the infirmary. Three of the brothers had been
laid low and with these three sick and the old men who
lived there, the infirmary beds were filled, so Brother
Francis and Brother Tom had been dispatched to find
another bed.

Father Peregrine spoke quietly to Brother Tom as
they came level with him: 'Brother Thomas, I shall need
you tonight. I have guests eating with me. Directly after
Vespers, please.'

'I'll be there!' replied Tom cheerily. 'Whoops! Mind
those flowers, Francis! Glory be to God, what are you
doing, man? It won't *bend*.'

'Move, then, I cannot get it into this passageway unless
you—NO, TOM that's my *hand*. Look, put it down a
minute. Now then, go back a bit. There!'

The journey with the bed through the gathering of
ancients in the herb garden, and the negotiation of the
doorways in the infirmary, had them doubled up with
laughter, nearly cost Francis the fingers of his left
hand, and vastly entertained the old men. They finally

brought it to rest, intact, in the right place, then stayed on to help Brother John take in the old men to their beds as the heat of the afternoon cooled and the shadows began to lengthen.

'Thanks, Brother,' said Brother John as he and Tom eased Brother Cyprian into his bed. 'Have you time to do one more thing for me? Brother Cyprian needs his medicine before supper. It takes a while to give it to him. Would you mind?'

He gave Brother Tom the bottle, and Tom bent over Brother Cyprian, coaxing him to take the physic, which eased the pain of his swollen, arthritic knees and helped him sleep. The medicine was syrupy and the spoon full. It required concentration to get it into, and keep it inside, the sunken mouth. Brother Tom was intent on the task and did not see the change in the old man's gaze from vacancy to shrewd observation.

Brother Cyprian swallowed convulsively and slowly wiped at his mouth with his shaky, blue-veined old hand. His eyes, bright with interest now, studied Brother Tom. 'I know thee, tha scoundrel,' he said. Brother Tom blinked at him in surprise. 'Aye, I do. I know the spark in thy eyes too: seen it many times. A womaniser and a thief, I'll wager, before tha came t'us, and now too, it wouldn't surprise me, give thee the chance.'

Tom was speechless, and Francis, approaching from across the room, heard the remark and laughed. 'You're absolutely right, Brother Cyprian, scoundrel he is. You know us all. It's the wisdom of God in you. Pray for him then, and the Lord Christ may make a saint of him yet.'

But Brother Cyprian was wandering again, and did not respond. The Vespers bell began to ring, and Tom straightened up, shaking his head. 'The old reprobate!'

'Reprobate yourself. It's true. He's seen that spark that's in your eye many times, he said so. Women I know nothing of, but light-fingered I can vouch for!'

He ducked the hand that shot out to cuff his ear and grinned affectionately at his friend; 'What's more, you'll be late for Vespers if we don't make haste. Brother John, are you coming?'

After Vespers the brothers ate together in the refectory. Then there was an hour of relaxation before Compline, when they were free to rest and converse, sitting in the community room which was lit by a fire in winter and the last rays of the evening sun now at the end of the summer.

Brother Cormac came in late from his last chores in the kitchen, to snatch a little company and conversation. He crossed the room to where Brother Tom and Brother Francis sat in dispute with Brother Giles and Brother Basil as to the best method of tickling trout. 'Ought you not to have been helping Father Abbot with his guests tonight, Tom?' Cormac asked in surprise.

Brother Tom froze in his seat and looked at Cormac, wide-eyed and utterly still. He took a deep breath. 'Holy saints! I forgot! Did no one stay from the kitchen when they took the food over?'

Cormac shook his head. 'No. They assumed you were on your way, I suppose.'

Tom gulped. 'He'll have my blood! He can't do a thing! Not pour the wine, nor serve them, nor even manage his own food. Oh I'm for it now.'

'Would his guests not help?' asked Brother Giles.

Tom shook his head. 'No, that's not the point. You know what our abbot is, as formal and particular as they come when it's a question of courtesy and hospitality. He'd as soon ask them to clean out the cows as pour the wine. Oh ... oh, how could I forget? Who are his guests, Cormac, do you know?'

Cormac grinned at him. 'Yes. I do. His guests are Sir Geoffrey and Lady Agnes d'Ebassier.'

Tom closed his eyes and groaned, then he opened them to stare hopelessly at Brother Cormac. 'What in the name of heaven am I going to do about this?' he asked.

'Could you not go over now?' suggested Brother Francis tentatively, but Tom withered him with a look. 'That would add insult to injury, I think. No, I'll just have to go and kiss the ground after Compline and hope he doesn't break my head with his crutch. Ah, by all that's holy, why me?'

They had no more heart for conversation, and after a few desultory exchanges sat in silence, listening to the anxious drumming of Tom's fingers on the side of the bench. And at last the sand in the hour glass ran out. Brother Basil got creakily to his feet and shuffled off to chapel to ring the Compline bell.

Father Peregrine walked to the guest house with his distinguished visitors.

'God give you good night, Sir Geoffrey, and my lady,' he said. 'It is an honour and a pleasure to be your host once more.'('And God forgive me the lie,' he added silently.) After exchanging a few more pleasantries, their conversation was ended by the ringing of the Office bell. Father Peregrine took his leave of them and set off for Compline. Lady Agnes lingered a moment to watch him go, then followed her husband in to the guest house.

'He is such a dear man,' she said dreamily as she closed the great oak door behind her, 'so courteous, but so natural. He makes one feel so at home; so ... wanted.' She paused a moment, then added wistfully, 'He truly listens.'

'What? Oh yes, good fellow,' barked Sir Geoffrey absently.

The dear man, meanwhile, was limping with angry jerks across the cloister towards the chapel, his mouth and jaw set hard.'I'll kill him. I'll kill him,' he was thinking.

He had waited and waited for Brother Tom to arrive after the lay servants from the kitchen had brought the food in dishes ready to be served, and departed leaving him stranded with his guests. Their visit, unannounced as it was, had found him rather unprepared, and he had not invited any of the brothers to eat with them, so there was no one to serve the food but himself and his two aristocratic guests. Eventually, unable to delay the meal any longer, he turned to Lady Agnes with a disarming smile and said 'Madam, I am in a little difficulty. Our brother who would normally wait upon us has evidently been detained. I would gladly wait upon you myself but ... as you see, I cannot. It distresses me to ask it, my lady, but I wonder—would you be so kind as to serve our food?'

Lady Agnes, having never lifted a finger to do anything for herself since the day she was born, was quite taken with the idea. Lifting the lids from the dishes, she sniffed with appreciation the fragrant steam, and proceeded gaily to serve the two men and herself.

Father Peregrine's heart sank as she placed before him a mighty portion of food. His head ached as if it would split open. Inwardly cursing his intended humility in having only one brother to wait upon him he smiled radiantly at Sir Geoffrey: 'My lord, could you— would you—I must ask you to pour our wine. I regret, that also is beyond me.'

'What? Oh, by all means, Father!' the baron blustered, embarrassed by Peregrine's disability and his own failure to notice the need. Father Peregrine put him at his ease with another dazzling smile, and they began their meal. They talked of this and that, Lady Agnes asking after various of the brothers, and Sir Geoffrey enlarging on his plans to stock his sister-in-law's larder with venison and fish as part of his holiday relaxation.

He was just in the middle of a long and tedious anecdote which was mainly designed to show off his prowess as a huntsman, when his wife interrupted him: 'I beg your pardon, my dear, for breaking in upon your story. Father, I am so sorry. I did not think. I can see you are having trouble with your meal. I hope you will not mind my asking—would you like me—will you permit me—to cut some of that meat for you?'

Sir Geoffrey cleared his throat and took a deep drink of his wine. 'Good stuff, this, very good,' he mumbled.

Peregrine looked at Lady Agnes, his face burning. Her eyes were fixed on him in anxious appeal, fearing that she had made an indiscretion. He smiled at her. It was the costliest smile of his life. 'That would be very good of you, my lady,' he said, 'the brother who waits on us would normally cut my food for me.'

Lady Agnes relaxed under the kindness of his smile, happy to have said the right thing after all.

'Do carry on with your story, dear,' she said. 'You were just saying how the boar broke suddenly from the undergrowth, right at your feet.'

'Ah, yes. Hmmph. Great big fellow. Glittering eyes and massive shoulders. Well, of course, there was only one thing to do. ...'

Peregrine submitted to having his food cut for him, and struggled to eat it, conscious of the lady's eyes on him, trying not to spill anything, trying to hurry, trying at the same time to convey rapt attention to the interminable tale, glad that at least somebody was talking and he did not have to think of anything to say himself.

All things come to an end, and the meal was over at last. Having taken his leave of Sir Geoffrey and Lady Agnes, he came in to Compline, trembling with fury and humiliation, sick with the throbbing pain in his head.

Brother Tom watched him come in. Father Peregrine did not so much as glance in Tom's direction, but sat down in his stall with elaborate composure, looking straight ahead, giving nothing away. Brother Tom, looking at the set line of his superior's mouth, was as apprehensive as he was remorseful.

The chant rose and fell in the shadows of the evening, lovely in its peace. The tranquillity of the Office concluded in the blessing, and the brothers slipped away in silence to their beds.

Father Peregrine remained where he was in his stall, looking straight ahead. He neither moved nor spoke as Brother Tom, who also stayed behind, stood reluctantly and walked slowly across the chapel to face him. Tom waited. At last Father Peregrine's gaze shifted to look him in the eye. Brother Tom looked down, unable to endure the anger that was turned on him.

'Where were you?' said Peregrine coldly.

Brother Tom looked up, but only for a pleading instant. His head bent, he mumbled almost inaudibly, 'I forgot. I just forgot. Oh, Father, I'm—'

'You *forgot*?' Peregrine leaned forward, shaking. 'You *forgot*? I have just spent the most humiliating and embarrassing evening of my life and you can come and face me here and tell me you just *forgot*? No, *don't* you kneel to me, I don't want to hear your apologies, Brother.'

'Father, I—'

'What was I supposed to do? I had to ask Lady Agnes to serve us at table and Sir Geoffrey to pour our wine. Brother, you—' He broke off, white with rage, glaring at poor Tom. 'Oh, go to your bed, get out of my sight,' he concluded, spitting out the words with biting anger.

Brother Tom turned to go, took two steps, but stopped and turned back again. He stood at the entrance to the abbot's stall a moment, and then knelt there before him. 'I cannot go,' he said miserably. 'It is the Rule, Father. The Rule for you as well as me. Do not let the sun go down on your anger. Be reconciled. I ... oh, Father, I'm sorry. I'll never, never do it again. Forgive me, I—'

'Again? *Again!* As I live, you will not! Brother Thomas—' He stopped and looked at him, Tom finding the courage somehow to meet his eyes. 'Can you not imagine what it is like to be imprisoned by these useless, useless hands? To be the object of the pity of those ... those ... of Sir Geoffrey and his wife?'

He shut his eyes and leaned back wearily in his stall. 'God forgives you, and so do I, Brother,' he said flatly, after a moment. 'Go to bed.'

But Tom, hesitantly, stretched out his hand, which was muscular and brown and workmanlike, with blunt, strong fingers. He closed it gently over Peregrine's hands.

'Please don't say useless,' he whispered. 'You don't know how ... ask Cormac, ask Theodore ... not useless ... so much I—I don't know how to say it, I ... no ... not useless. Oh, Father, I'm sorry.'

But his abbot did not move or speak, and Tom withdrew his hand and crept wretchedly to bed.

Peregrine sat, completely still, weary and frustrated as the anger ebbed away. The events of the day flowed through his mind. He thought of Brother Cyprian: 'Tha thought thyself a king on thy throne. Knocked thee off, did they?' Of Lady Agnes, smiling, happily and inexpertly dismembering a fat roast fowl, and the touch of Tom's hand on his own, 'Not useless ... not useless. ...'

He opened his eyes. The chapel was all but dark now, but he could still make out the shape of the figure on the great cross.

'What imprisons me, then? My hands or my pride?' he thought sadly. He remembered his words to Tom: 'The most humiliating and embarrassing evening of my life. ...' Gazing at the cross, he shook his head. He thought of Jesus, blindfolded by the soldiers, beaten and mocked. 'Prophesy then, prophet! Which of us hit you?' Father Peregrine groaned in his shame and bent over, burying his face in his mutilated hands.

'Oh ... oh, Brother Thomas, forgive my pride,' he murmured. Holy Jesus, crucified one, if my hands are useless, what are yours? Oh ... oh no ... forgive. ...'

After a while he straightened himself and sat looking at the dim shape of the cross, emptied and tired.

'Aggravating, strutting peacock ...' Brother Cyprian's words came back to him, and he began to smile. 'Amen,' he said, ruefully.

He stood up, bowed in reverence to the real presence of Christ, and went to his bed.

In the morning, Brother Tom came to shave him, after the morning Office of Prime, and was much relieved to be greeted with the usual friendliness. He stood at the table, assembling soap and blade and water, while Father Peregrine sat in his chair and waited. After he had been waiting a few moments, struck by the intense quietness, he turned his head to look at Brother Tom. He watched with curiosity as Tom stood very still, the linen towel in his hand, his eyes closed.

'What are you doing?' said Father Peregrine.

Brother Tom started guiltily and opened his eyes. 'I—I was praying,' he said, flushing slightly as Peregrine continued to look enquiringly at him; 'I was praying I'd not cut you.'

Father Peregrine burst out laughing. 'Oh, forgive me, Brother! Am I so intimidating? It was in haste and anger I spoke last night. My pride was wounded.' As Tom tucked the towel round his neck, Peregrine leaned back in the chair looking up at him. 'My pride can do with some denting,' he said quietly. 'Oh, but Brother—for the love of God, don't forget again.'

Brother Tom bent over him, and shaved him carefully—it was quite an art shaving that scarred face—then dried Peregrine's face and throat and stood back to survey his handiwork.

'Brother Cyprian', said Peregrine with a wry smile, 'described me yesterday as an aggravating, strutting peacock. He said I thought of myself as a king on his throne.'

Brother Tom grinned as he contemplated him. 'Well, I'll not tell you what he called me! There, you look beautiful, my lord. I'll clear these things away now and be gone. I'll see you at the midday meal. Without fail, I stake my life.'

It was with a sense of sweet relief that Father Peregrine bid God speed to his guests after the noon meal, and he stood in the abbey courtyard to watch them go, his hand raised to his eyes against the sunshine, absorbing the still, gentle warmth of the mid-September afternoon. Then he let his hand fall and made his way slowly to the infirmary, where Brother Michael worked on his hands for a while with the aromatic oils. Father Peregrine closed his eyes and relaxed. After all these years, the sensations in his hands were still odd; they were in places numb, in others tingling or painful to touch. Still, all in all it was a soothing and comforting thing, Brother Michael's quietness and the gentle firmness of his touch.

'Father, I beg your pardon—' Peregrine opened his eyes at the sound of Brother James' apologetic voice. 'I'm sorry, but another visitor has arrived and is asking to see you.'

'Oh, no!' he groaned. 'Oh, Brother, no! Who is it?'

'It's a woman with a little baby—I forget the exact name she gave. A Melissa Langforth? Thornton? Something like—'

'Melissa!' Father Peregrine's face lit with happiness and he snatched his hand out of Brother Michael's and, stooping, fumbled on the floor for the crutch that lay beside him. 'She's my—she's my—she's a relative of mine,' he said to Brother James as he limped out of the room with jerky haste to find her.

She was walking down the cobbled path to meet him, and she laughed at his eagerness and joy as he greeted her.

'Welcome, daughter, oh welcome! We heard your joyful news, dear heart, but I never thought to see you so soon. So this is the littlest, a son. Bless him, look at that yawn! By the saints, what a great, cavernous mouth he has on him! And a roar like a lion, I'll be bound. But come, dearest, let me find you a place in the guest house where you can rest and be comfortable. You must be mortally weary; you should not have travelled so soon. Would to God that all our visitors were as welcome as you!'

She stayed with them for a week, and she would sit in the gardens outside the infirmary, her baby on her knee, talking to Uncle Edward, and the old brothers who sat out in the sun with him, and to Peregrine when he could snatch the time. It was one of those brief spells of complete happiness that come once in a rare while, an unlooked-for gift of God, when the forces of darkness, of sorrow and temptation seem miraculously held back, a breathing-space in the battle.

On the third day of her visit, Peregrine stole an afternoon to be with her, and they sat together in the deepening golden peace of the afternoon sun, Melissa suckling her child and telling all the news from home.

She lifted up the baby, drunken and replete, eyes drowsing shut, a dribble of white milk trickling from his slack mouth. Holding him up to her with his head nestled on her shoulder, she stroked his back as they talked. The baby gave a huge, satisfied belch, which made them all smile.

'Father, would you like to hold him?' she said.

Peregrine looked at her, and looked down at his hands, and then at Melissa again, and the wistfulness and sadness in his eyes went through her like a knife.

'Of course you can hold him!' she exclaimed. 'Here, I'll lay him on your lap, so; rest his head on your hand.' Gently she straightened Peregrine's fingers under the downy head. The baby looked up at him, and gurgled and smiled—the little, confiding noises of baby conversation, the endearing, dimpled, toothless smile of innocent happiness.

Peregrine gently stroked the delicate skin of the child's forehead, smiling back at his grandson, his face radiant with vulnerable tenderness.

'Thus was Jesus,' he whispered, 'and thus all the little ones whom Herod butchered. Oh, God protect you in this world, dear one. God keep you safe from harm.'

Melissa watched the tiny, pink hand grip round Peregrine's scarred, twisted fingers, and sadness welled up in her for sorrow to come, for the inevitable harshness and pain.

'You can't ask that, Father, and you know it, of all people,' she said gently. 'But let him travel through life with his hand gripping Jesus' scarred hand as tight as it now grips yours, and the storms will not vanquish him.'

The baby yawned hugely, and Peregrine looked up at Melissa, delighted. 'Wearied by theology, God save him, at eight weeks old! Oh Melissa, you have brought me joy!'

She came and stood beside him, leaning against him, her arm resting around his neck, her fingertips stroking absently, tracing the scar on his face as she smiled down at her baby son.

'It's a wonderful, wonderful, sacred thing; this perfect little life, a new beginning born out of my body, out of Ranulf's and my love. It must be hard, to live without family life. Did you never think you missed your way, maybe, being a monk?'

'Missed my way? No, not me. Did I choose it, or did God choose me? I would make the same choice again tomorrow. Although ... sometimes my skin is hungry for tenderness of touch as you touch me now. Yes, that I miss: but no one is guaranteed that loving tenderness, and look, I have found it in the cloister, where others starve for it among their own kin, at their own hearthside.'

A sudden grimace of distress crossed the baby's face, and he opened his gums wide in a trembling cry of protest. Melissa stooped and lifted him, held him against her, patting and rocking him gently. He drew his knees up and cried again, then belched enormously, and relaxed, content.

'He is not yet baptised, Father. I saved that for you. Will you baptise him for me this week?'

'Need you ask? I am honoured! Benedict, you said you were naming him, did you not? What brought that on?'

'Well I wanted him to be named after you, but Peregrine is such an outlandish, ridiculous name, and none of the brothers here ever call you Columba—your kitchen brother says you may coo over the baby, but you're still no dove. So I didn't know what to choose. But I've been reading the Rule of Life that St Benedict wrote, and all he says the abbot should be sounds just like you, so I thought Benedict would do, because his Rule has shaped your life.'

Peregrine said nothing for a moment. She could not read his expression. His eyes were very bright in his lean, intent face as he looked at her.

'That is all right, isn't it?' she said.

'Yes. Oh yes. I was just a bit overcome by the compliment you've just paid me. There, Brother Basil is ringing the Vespers bell.' He raised his voice. 'Wake up, Edward!'

Brother Edward started awake from his peaceful doze.

'Eh? What is it? Vespers already? Forgive me, Melissa, sleeping. My old age overwhelms what manners I ever had, these days.'

He yawned and stood slowly. The three of them walked together up the cobbled path, Melissa holding her baby close and peaceful against her: four generations. At the guest house they parted company, and Melissa went in to lay her drowsy baby in his bed.

Peregrine and Edward continued together to the chapel.

'God has been so generous to me, Edward. The sin of my youth is covered by his forgiving love, and all that is left of it is his gift of a daughter, and grandchildren. His generosity is more than I can comprehend.'

They entered together the cool dimness of the chapel and went each to his own stall.

Motes of dust floated in the rays of sun that slanted through the narrow windows. The brothers' voices lifted in the sixty-second psalm. Peregrine closed his eyes and allowed his soul to be lifted on the beauty of the chant. 'Is this worship,' he wondered, 'or is it self-indulgence?'

He joined in the singing of the sixty-third psalm: '*Quoniam melior est misericordia tua super vitas, labia mea laudabunt te* ...—For your loving-kindness is better than life itself: my lips shall speak your praise ...'

He opened his eyes, and his gaze fell on the great wooden crucifix, and then his attention was caught by a movement. Brother James, the newest of the new generation of novices, was still struggling with endless rules and regulations, and was creeping in late, standing wretchedly with downcast eyes, in the place of shame set apart for late-comers. Little darts of disapproval were flying his way from Father Matthew, who had seen him, too. Ah, well, life goes on ...

'*Quia fuisti adjutor meus. Et in velamento alarum tuarum exultabo* ...—Because you have been my helper, therefore in the shadow of your wings I rejoice ...'

'Bear up, Brother James, three months now and you'll be professed, God willing, and then it will be me you have to deal with, and not Father Matthew. God grant I may not be over-indulgent with you, because you *are* undisciplined for all your heart's in the right place ...'

Father Matthew, perfecting his withering look at the unfortunate Brother James, flared his nostrils and inhaled more dust than he had bargained for, which caused him to sneeze, violently. Peregrine lowered his head, glad that the cowl hid his face, burying his delighted grin in the pages of his breviary:

'*Gloria Patri et Filio, et Spiritui Sancto* ...'

Repentantly, Peregrine composed his face, and gave his attention to the prayers. Wise old Benedict had laid down in his Rule of Life that at the first Office of the day and in the evening at Vespers, the abbot should pray aloud the Lord's Prayer, so that the day should begin and end with the remembrance that we are forgiven, and must in our turn forgive, and so all differences between the brethren be laid to rest.

Abbot Peregrine raised his head and led the prayer in his firm, clear voice:

'*Pater noster, qui es in caelis, sanctificetur nomen tuum* ...'

Then the Office was ended, and the brothers were

dispersing quietly. Brother James came and knelt before Peregrine, humbly awaiting penance.

'Say a *Miserere*, my son, and try to be in good time tomorrow,' said Father Peregrine mildly.

Then with a light heart he set on his way to meet Melissa and Brother Edward at his house for supper, and smiled at the sight of Brother Tom, hastening ahead of him, anxious not to be late.

'And that's all,' said Mother firmly, looking at the clock. 'There were plenty of other stories, though, to keep us going in the New Year.'

She smiled and stretched and yawned, and uncurled reluctantly from her armchair.

'Bed time, I think, my darling. Happy New Year.'

We took one candle to light our way upstairs, and blowing out the other one, left the dying fire, its embers faintly illuminating the night.

Shivering in the unheated bedroom, I decided it was too cold to wash and clean my teeth, so I slipped off my dressing-gown and crept quietly into my bed, careful not to disturb my sleeping sisters. It was warm and cosy under the blankets; Therese had left me the hot-water bottle there. I lay for a long time in the darkness, listening to my sisters' regular, peaceful breathing, punctuated by the little sighs and murmurs of sleep: thinking, remembering, imagining ... and then finally thinking drifted into dreaming, and I was asleep.

Those are some of the stories then, that Mother told me the year I turned fifteen, so many years ago now: stories of my long ago grandfather, Peregrine du Fayel, and his Uncle Edward, and his daughter Melissa, named for Melissa du Fayel, Peregrine's mother. Down the ladder of seven hundred years they have climbed, preserved by grandmother and mother and daughter, told at the firesides of our family through all those generations. My mother, my wonderful, magical mother, weaver of dreams, with her dark, compelling eyes, her wild mane of hair, and the soft blue folds of her skirt: she made them come alive for me, and they fed my hungry soul, and they changed everything for me. They have been stored away in the garden of my imagination, walled away since I was a young girl, until I have opened the green door and taken you in to wander in the garden. And the stories were there waiting, surprisingly fresh to my memory after all. ... Well, but Peregrine was unforgettable, wasn't he? So now I have told some of them to you. I hope, I really hope, they fed your hunger too. I wish you had known my mother, for she would have told them better than I; but there it is. Like you, I make the best of what I can do.